LILY

BOOK TWO

IN OUR MOTHER'S GARDEN

By

Joyce Humphrey Cares

Mainstream Romance

I Heart Book Publishing, LLC

enjoy the magic
Joyce

Lily
Book Two, In Our Mother's Garden

Copyright © 2017 Joyce Humphrey Cares

First E-book Publication: August 2017

Cover design by Dawné Dominique
Edited by Sherri Good
All interior design and logo Copyright © 2017 by I Heart
Book Publishing, LLC

ISBN: 978-1-9740-3830-5

First Print Edition: August 2017

10 9 8 7 6 5 4 3 2 1

DEDICATION

To My sons Eric and Mark

BACK COVER

Fulfilling a dream, Lily O'Malley moves to Paris, France, a place she has always wanted to live. After a busy year of settling in, a vacation is much needed. She makes up her mind to visit her college roommate who lives in Warsaw, Poland.

She has always denied being clairvoyant. However, riding on the night train from Paris to Warsaw, she experiences an unexplained vision – her first in many years. She is drawn into the dark past of another time – the era the Nazis occupied Poland during World War II.

Facing frightening situations, she meets a handsome stranger, French Diplomat, Pierre Girard, who fights with and trains Polish resistance workers. She wants to become involved with the effort to help rescue the Jews and others the Nazis consider to be undesirable. Pierre flies Lily to London, England to train to be anything needed to defeat the German enemy.

As a witness to the ravaged landscape, treachery and violence of World War II and the 1940s in Poland, she travels from the Baltic Sea to the Tatra Mountains with the Partisans. Lily knows she will always remember the people she worked to save from the concentration camps and death and the friends she made. She refuses to concentrate on the bad memories competing for the space the good ones are trying to occupy.

LILY

When Lily O'Malley visits Poland, the door to the past is ripped open...Transported back to the 1940's, she experiences the horrors of World War II.

PROLOGUE

September 1, 1939-Poland

The day was clear and warm. Dusk on its way to darkness was about to surround the citizens of Poland and very soon after that other European countries. The spread of evil was perpetrated essentially by one person, Adolf Hitler. The rise of Adolf Hitler and his henchmen was one of the most terrible and unbelievable stories in the history of the world. These men marched over lowlands, highlands, and mountains.

Hitler's hatred of the Jewish race was an obsession. Jews over twelve years of age had to wear a Star of David on their clothes. Their bank accounts were seized. Their houses and businesses were confiscated. Hospitals and schools were denied to them. Their Synagogues were closed. Finally, the Jews and others considered undesirable were forced into ghettos and not allowed to leave under punishment of death.

When Hitler became the leader of Germany, he mobilized criminal elements who beat up his enemies.

They became a paramilitary organization, the "brown shirts" named after their all-brown uniforms. He took hoodlums, gave them a brown shirt with an armband sporting a swastika, taught them the Nazi salute, and handed them each a stick to beat others. Once he got absolute power no one controlled him. Hitler managed to erase millions of the Jews throughout Europe.

He began his destruction and World War II with a Blitzkrieg. Tanks, the Luftwaffe dropping bombs, foot soldiers, and the cavalry stormed into Poland, surprising the residents, from three directions the north, east, and south. World War II began September 1, 1939.

After the shock of what was happening to them subsided, the Poles formed resistance groups, home army units, and Partisans. They worked together to fight the demon. They covered back roads, the woods, and eventually roads within the city limits. They blew up trains and sabotaged factories manufacturing war machines for the German war efforts, worked wireless radios, and helped men and women escape the country and prisoners break out of the death camps before it was their time to enter the gas chamber.

When she read of the women who made a difference in World War II, the story of the Holocaust fascinated Lily O'Malley. Once she began to read the stories and diaries of the women, it was hard for her to not stop reading until she reached the last page.

The women fought like men. Some women became leading figures in the resistance. They trained in London, England, for eight months with the Special Operations Executive — SOE — and MI6. After their training, they parachuted back into Poland and other countries of their origins helping hundreds of Jews and enemy soldiers escape.

Women, because they were considered the weaker sex, were able to run circles around the Gestapo. The secret police employing underhanded and terrorist methods in the Nazi regime. Some of these women even topped the Gestapo's most-wanted list. Although a few were captured and severely tortured, when caught by the German SS, the men who wore black uniforms and were in charge of intelligence and espionage, they never gave up their fellow resistance workers. A couple of the women sentenced to death managed to evade execution by bribing a guard.

During the war, leaves turned the glorious colors of red, yellow, and orange in the warm fall and crunched under foot when they fell from the trees. Then a foggy humid period morphing into a snowy winter came. Soon shortages of wood and food followed. The enemy and allies huddled in front of fires and made the best of what they had. After a few months, a warm and sunny spring and summer arrived. Green leaves filled the tree branches. Birds mated, raising their young in their nests. Bees hovered over flowers and butterflies flitted through the gardens.

The season's progressed year after year. The war waged on. The Germans trampled over Poland and through Europe leaving a wake of destruction and death in their path. The gruesome scenes would never be forgotten.

CHAPTER ONE

October 1, 2014 – the train to Poland

"All aboard." Lily heard the conductor yell as she slung her purse over her shoulder. After handing her suitcase to the porter, she grabbed the small case sitting beside her on the platform, climbed the stairs, and walked down the corridor of the general seating to the first class compartments. Looking through the windows at the passengers, who had already settled down in their private sections of the train, she smiled. She also glanced at the numbers on the doors. "130, 131, 132, here I am. 132." Stopping at her compartment, she stood in front of the huge window across the corridor from her door and pulled it down. She leaned out and waved goodbye to her boss as the high-speed night train pulled out of Paris Nord Train Station. The trip would take her to Frankfurt, Germany, to Berlin, Germany, and to her final destination the Warsaw Central Station in Poland—a fourteen-hour trip. It wasn't quite dark, but the sky was colored in pinks and purples as the sunlight dimmed and the lights of the station flicked on.

The train pulled away and picked up speed as it left the Paris Nord railway station. The station grew smaller. When she lost sight of her editor and the lights, she pushed up the window and turned toward her compartment. A quick glance in the glass window of her door before pulling it open revealed her slender body and slim hips, delicately carved facial bones, and a nose exquisitely dainty. Her strawberry blonde hair hung past her shoulders and her green eyes were the color of emeralds. After pushing down on the handle of the door and pulling on it, Lily opened it immediately.

She fell into the well-padded, leather bench. Tossing her purse and small case on the seat next to her, she rested against the back of the bench, propped her feet on the seat, tucking them under her, and stared out of the window while waiting for her checked larger case to be delivered to her compartment.

As she listened to the whine of the high-speed train flying on the tracks, she thought about leaving Bar Harbor, Maine. After graduating from college with a major in Journalism, she packed her belongings and moved to Paris, the City of Light. The place she had always wanted to live, since visiting the glorious city with her parents on one of their buying trips for their antique shop. She knew then she would live there one day.

After she landed in Paris, she found a studio apartment on the left bank of the Seine River. Waiting for her belongings to be shipped to her, she began her job search. Her dream of writing International news and an editorial once in a while was set aside after several weeks. The only position she could find was as editor of the food section in a small Paris paper.

Realizing the rent had to be paid, she took the job writing restaurant reviews, recipes, family holiday traditions, seasonal food, and wines. Soon she enjoyed both her job and her apartment. The job she had was the right one for her after all, and she worked hard at it. In her free time, she decorated her small living area, six hundred square feet. Her neighbor, the sister of a French diplomat, showed her little stores on the back streets of the left bank where she found a lot of furniture, accent pillows, curtains, and knickknacks that made her home comfy. For her, a walk on the banks of the river was an enjoyable afternoon entertainment. She even bought a few paintings to decorate the walls by artists who gathered on the banks of the Seine and painted scenes of Paris.

The neighbor, whose family consisted of her brother and great-grandfather, promised to introduce Lily to her brother, who was in New York City for a year as ambassador, when he came back to Paris. Lily saw his photo. He was someone she wanted to be introduced to. The year couldn't come fast enough. She looked forward to their meeting.

In Paris for six months, she worked herself into the job of senior editor of the food section. Her attempt to develop new and interesting columns was successful. The goal to make her section the best in the paper succeeded. The food section became the reason people bought the paper. Her boss finally told her he didn't want her to burn out and to take a vacation.

He is right. Lily emailed her college roommate, Rachel, who went home to Poland after graduation from college and arranged a visit.

A knock on her door jolted her out of her reverie. "Yes."

A porter slid the door open and stared at her. "Your large case, Madam. Shall I put it on the rack above the seat?"

"Yes, but just a minute. I need to get something out of the front pocket first."

She unzipped the outer pocket of the case and pulled out her laptop. "Okay, it can go up now," she said getting out of his way as she set the computer on the seat and watched him turn to leave the compartment.

"Wait." Pulling a few euros from her purse, she pressed them into his hand.

"Merci." He smiled a wide grin. "Just push the button over the sink if you need anything."

"Thank you. I will." She smiled.

Glancing out the window, she watched the scenery zoom by. *I'm glad I decided on the train as opposed to flying. It is much more relaxing and there is more room.* Squeezing herself into the small space around a seat on an airplane was not how she wanted to start her vacation. *I need to relax.* She slid off her jacket and threw it next to her on the seat. *There will be time to write my column and email it to my editor before I reached my destination. I know once I see Rachel there will be no time to write. I'll be dragged all around Eastern Europe. I want to make sure the column goes into the Sunday edition.*

Opening her laptop as she sat, she thought about her experience when she attended the opening of the quaint café in Montmartre, Boutay and began to type. She could smell the aromas of the spices and herbs they served with their special fish entrees, as she wrote.

Finished with her column, she leaned back, reread what she wrote, added a typed note to her editor asking him to go into her office computer and add a picture of the restaurant. Finished, she pushed send. Before she closed her computer, she typed a short note to her college roommate.

I'm on my way, Rachel. It was so nice of you to agree to have me visit for a few weeks. My boss at the paper gave me the vacation days as long as I write about Polish food and send my articles to him while I'm here. I could barely hide my excitement.

I ran home and packed before he changed his mind. Can't wait to see you. Love L.

The last thing she typed was her arrival time. Pressing send, she closed the laptop. Standing on the seat, she returned her computer to the outside pocket of her stowed suitcase. Then she jumped down reached for the curtain over the window and drew it closed. Yawning, she leaned forward, reached into the closet across from where she sat and pulled out a blanket and pillow. She tugged off her boots, dropping them in front of the cabinet she had just closed then curled up on the seat, tucking her feet underneath her. Reaching above her head, she pushed the switch and flicked off the light. She fluffed up the pillow laying it at the end of the seat near the door. Stretching the blanket over her, she closed her eyes and nodded off.

October, 1939-Poland

Lily jumped, sitting straight up when a loud crack and then a rumbling noise of thunder awoke her. It was hard for her to erase the cobwebs of sleep, so she turned the water faucets on in the small sink and splashed water on her face.

She turned toward the outside window, pulled it down, and stared out. A bolt of lightning fractured the dark clouds in the sky. Raindrops hit the lower part of the window. Fog crept through the opening. It filled her compartment. Trying to see if she could recognize where she was, she stood close to the window and stuck out her head. The scenery was hidden by the fog, but she enjoyed letting the raindrops hit her face. The cool breeze created by the speeding train felt good.

Finally, she realized her face wasn't the only part of her that was getting wet. Quickly, she pulled in her head and pushed the window closed. She reached over to the sink next to the closet, flicked on the light over the small basin, and looked into the mirror. With wet cheeks and hair, she grabbed the towel hanging from the wall rack to dry them. Raising her arm, she squinted as she glanced at her watch. It was midnight.

"Wait. My clothes." *What is going on?* The image she saw as she glanced at herself in the mirror was confusing. Her jeans and sweater had been replaced by a blouse and wrinkled skirt. Its hemline fell just below her knees. Stockings had been switched from the socks she wore. The wedged heeled pumps on her feet were uncomfortable. With second thoughts and after kicking them off, she bent down and moved them away from the seat. As she neatly lined them up near the closet, she noticed a dark seam running up the back of her nylon stockings. *I would never wear clothes like these. I don't understand. They aren't even in style.*

Startled, she heard the clanking of the train wheels on the tracks and the sound of a steam engine. She shut off the light leaving the compartment in the dark. Turning toward the window, she saw rain drops no longer hit the pane. The weather had cleared. With a quick move to the window, she pulled it down again, far enough this time, so she was able to stick her head and shoulders out.

Twisting side to side, she looked at the front and back of the train. Smoke from the engine flowed past and back to the end of the train, flowing into the night. As the cars followed a curve in the tracks, she saw the engineer shoveling coal into a boiler filled with red coals. Yellow flames jumped out of the furnace. *What's going on?* Her search of the scenery as the train moved on the tracks, made her uneasy. The smoke and rocking of the train made it hard for her to see what the scenery was like.

The train slowed and slid to a stop. She reached up and pulled back the curtain covering the door window of her compartment and saw a railroad station. A man and woman sat on a bench outside of the wooden building of the depot. They picked up their luggage and walked to a back compartment and general sitting.

Walking from her compartment to the outside hallway, she opened the window and craned her neck. A group of soldiers and a man in a long black raincoat with a fedora hat pulled low on his forehead stood under a sign above the station door. It read *Berlin*. Several men dressed in black Jackboots, brown military style shirts, and red armbands searched under all the cars of the train. A shiver crept up her back as she pulled the window up and slammed it shut. A chill climbed her back. Afraid the men would see her watching them, she quickly turned, opened her door, and dropped down on the seat. With the light shut off, she looked around and tried to figure out what was going on.

A loud knock on her compartment door distracted her. A tall, blond-haired, blue-eyed soldier stood outside her door in the dimly lighted hall. He was dressed in brown like the men searching the grounds of the station. Quickly, she stood, grabbed the door knob, and pulled on it. As she threw open the door, it wasn't hard to miss his red armband with the black swastika on a white circle. It stood out even in the dim light.

When she flicked on the switch inside the door, the room lit up like it was filled with exploding fireworks. Bending, she peered around the floor for her shoes. Her hands were shaking. Fear knotted inside her. *Where did I put my shoes? Okay, here they are.* She had forgotten she placed them in front of the closet door. She grabbed and slipped them on as the man in front of her waited. Her hands began to shake when she saw the deep furrows creasing his forehead and his finger tapping on the door jam. She quickly backed away from him.

"Papers." He glared at her as he edged into the doorway.

Her pulse began to race. *What's going on?* Wordlessly, her stomach churned. Their eyes met. Shock caused her words to wedge in her throat. *What is he talking about?*

"Papers." This time he yelled as he pushed into her space. His stare drilled through her.

All right, let's see. Where would my papers be? Maybe… Reaching behind her, she picked up her purse, pulling out her passport. Her hands still shook, as she handed it to him. *I hope this will satisfy him.* She waited while he opened the passport, studying each page as he turned them. A cold knot formed in her stomach. Increasingly uneasy, she felt as if a hand closed around her throat, cutting off her breath. Finally taking a large gulp, she sucked in her breath and summoned up the courage as casually as she could to ask what was going on outside.

"Some escaped prisoners. Nothing to worry about. Are you traveling alone, Madame?" He glared at her.

"Yes." As her eyes met his, she felt a shock run through her.

"Where are you going?" He scanned her passport again.

"To Poland to visit a friend." Disconcerted, she crossed her arms and pointedly looked away. Beginning to calm down, her breathing became easier for her.

"You're coming from France. It's a good thing you're traveling while you still can."

"What do you mean?"

"Our troops will be moving over Europe. Very soon we will be in France and in control. We Germans will rule the world."

He handed back her passport then raised his right arm sticking it out in a salute as he backed out of the compartment. "Have a safe trip. Heil Hitler."

She watched him click his heels together and slide the door shut. With hesitation, she raised her right arm half-heartedly, not matching his enthusiastic gesture. Her lower lip trembled as she forced a smile. A shiver flowed through her as he continued on down the corridor. A soft gasp escaped her when she heard him repeat the same question at the next compartment.

She pulled down the door shade and dropped onto the train seat. Slumping against the back of the bench, she tried to figure out what was going on. Laying down, she propped her feet on her purse and case, and pulled the blanket around her, eventually falling asleep.

October 1, 2014

Awoken by a voice yelling "Warsaw Central Station, twenty minutes," she heard the porter knock when he passed her compartment as he strolled down the hallway outside the cabins announcing the first stop in Poland.

She heard his knock again on her door as he walked back to the front of the train. "Your stop, Miss. Ten minutes."

"Thanks," she yelled back as she threw off her blanket.

Lily gazed down at her clothes. They were back, the ones she wore when she boarded the train. To make sure, she checked again in the mirror. Jeans, shirt. Right. Lily rubbed her eyes. *Things are back to normal.* Her boots were where she had dropped them. Jumping off the seat, she squeezed the paste from next to the sink on her toothbrush. Opening her purse, she grabbed her hair brush, pulled it through her hair, then splashed her face with water and dried it. Her makeup was last. With a glance around to make sure everything was packed, she pulled up the window shade of her compartment.

Using her hand to keep the bright sun from shining in her eyes, as its rays bounced off the mirror and sent sparkling dots scattering helter-skelter through the room, she turned away from the window, folded the blanket, stuffed her things into her case, and slid the door of her compartment open. Dragging her suitcase off the shelf above her head, she set it on the floor beside her. Her purse and smaller case were carried in one hand.

"Here, let me help you."

Lily looked behind her as the porter reached for her large case.

"Thank you." She smiled. "I didn't realize you had come back. It's ready to go."

Followed by him, she walked unsteadily toward the exit. The train rocked as it slowed and finally stopped.

"Be careful, Miss."

"I'm fine now. The train has stopped," she said over her shoulder. Holding onto the rail, she stepped down to the platform. Squinting into the bright sunlight, she waited for the porter to join her. When he set her case beside her, she set her other bag down to reach into her purse, and then pressed another generous tip into his hand. He grinned as he nodded thank you and left her standing at the station. She searched in her purse for her sunglasses. Finding them, she slid them to the bridge of her nose.

When she heard her name called, she looked in the direction of the voice.

"Lily, Lily."

She saw her friend rushing down the station platform toward her. "Rachel," she yelled, waving back.

"Lily, I'm so glad I wasn't late. The traffic was terrible. Everyone is headed for the country for the weekend," she cried out as she reached Lily.

Rachel stared at her friend. "You haven't changed one ounce, Lily. You're still thin and fit. Are you still working out?"

Rachel gave her a hug.

"No. I haven't had much time since I moved to Paris. I think I may have put on a few pounds."

"Well, it looks good on you."

"You haven't changed either, Rachel. It's so good to see you. How long has it been?" Lily asked.

"Too long." Rachel hugged her friend. "Did you have breakfast? You aren't skipping breakfast like you did in college are you?"

"No. I'm hooked on bread and Parisian sweet rolls. Have them every morning. I must have slept through the announcement of breakfast. I didn't sleep very well at the beginning of the night but finally fell asleep toward morning."

"Come on. Before we start to our vacation home, we'll stop for coffee and something sweet. There's a little café around the corner." She pulled up the handle of Lily's large case and talked as they walked. "It's a beautiful day. We'll sit outside. Grab a table. You watch your cases. I'll get the coffee and rolls."

"Make my coffee black," Lily called to her friend as she saw her run into the shop.

Looking around, she found a table in the shade under an awning and sat. She slipped her sunglasses to the end of her nose as she watched two elderly men sitting at the next table playing chess. Noticing one man looked extremely pleased with himself as he moved his piece, she grinned. *He must be winning.* Turning, she pulled off her sunglasses and hooked them over the top button of her blouse.

"Can I help?" Lily asked as Rachel approached the table carrying a tray.

"No, thanks." Rachel set down the tray in front of the empty place at the table.

"The sweets look good."

"We're going to have a great visit. Karl won't be joining us until next weekend. His government work keeps him very busy. He's going to stay in the city at our apartment so we'll have lots of time to catch up." Rachel took the paper plate with two sweet rolls and the cups of coffee off the tray. Smiling, she dropped into the seat. "They're both the same mixed with spices and icing on top. Here's your coffee." Rachel pushed a paper cup toward Lily.

"Thanks. Let me put the tray on the table behind us. It's empty."

"Lily, why didn't you sleep? The motion of the train puts me right into dreamland." Her friend's smile broadened.

"That's it. I did nothing but dream. The dreams were not very sweet. They were creepy."

"This part of the world has a great deal of history and not a very nice history. I have a bad dream once in a while. We'll do some sightseeing while you're here. I'll show you some of the horrors of World War II. Then you will see how bad dreams can be." Rachel balled her napkin and stuffed it into her paper cup. "Are you finished?"

"I loved the rolls, but they were very sticky." Lily licked her fingers, wiping them dry with the napkin. "Yes. I'm finished." Popping the last bit of her roll into her mouth, she decided not to talk about her dreams until they got to the house. "I'll tell you about what I dreamt later." First, she wanted to watch the scenery and find out what her friend had been up to as they drove.

"Let's get started. My car is parked in the next block. Give me your case."

"I'm okay. I can manage it." With the handle pulled up, she slipped the strap of her purse over her shoulder. "I guess you can take the small one." Lily followed her friend. "You still walk very fast." Suddenly remembering, she was always two steps behind Rachel when they went anywhere she picked up the pace.

Lily heard Rachel pop the trunk open with a button on her key chain. With both hands, she lifted her case into the trunk and watched her friend slip the small case beside it.

Lily slid into the passenger seat as she heard Rachel slam the trunk lid shut. Barely closing her door, she stared as Rachel slipped into her seat, started up the car, and maneuvered into traffic. Once she settled her purse on the floor, she slipped her seat buckle into its slot. The vista of the inner-city's modern buildings and small gardens sitting in the middle of a group of houses, as her friend sped along its streets, were pleasant to look at.

"I feel as if I'm on a race track."

"I have to keep up with the traffic. I'll slow down as soon as we get out of town. We'll be out of here in a few minutes and on country roads," Rachel said. "It's a nice ride. You'll enjoy the scenery."

"I already do. The city is very beautiful." Lily relaxed and soon began to enjoy the Polish countryside. They sped through endless greenery, fruit trees, flower's growing wild, animals in the meadows, the sounds of crickets singing, and small villages with stone or concrete block homes. The tree's leaves were in full fall colors of red, yellow, and orange, as were the flowers. Their conversation skipped from topic to topic like two schizophrenics with flights of ideas.

"I bet you think I have every minute planned," Rachel said. "Well, I don't. The only thing I have arranged is a Chopin concert. It's a benefit for the World War Two Holocaust survivors and those who died in the Warsaw Ghetto, and they will be honored at the concert."

"When is it?"

"We have to come back into town on Wednesday."

"I'm all yours, except for one thing."

"And what is that?"

"I would like to take a cooking class and learn some local recipes. I promised my editor I would do a column on Polish cooking for the paper while I'm here. I saw the advertisement for one course online. As I remember, it's on Thursday morning at the chef's cooking school."

"Good. We can stay in town Wednesday night and go back to the country on Thursday after the class. I just might take it with you. I need to do some cooking. My housekeeper is getting rather elderly, and I need to take over some of her duties around the house. I feel cooking is one I should start doing. Standing in the kitchen for long periods of time is bad for her legs." She smiled. "As you might remember I never was a very good cook."

Lily laughed. "Yes, I remember the dinner you made when we double dated on Valentine's Day just before I left for home. The table decoration were beautiful, red hearts, flowers, and candles, but all the food burned. We had to order in pizza."

"Yes. My date was Karl. Can you believe it? Even though I've known him since we were children, we were friendly with different groups of friends, but my bad cooking didn't faze him. He invited me out on a date again and married me."

"You're very good at planning a party and decorating, Rachel. You just have to order in the food."

"You were always good at making elaborate food. Everyone at our parties wanted your recipes. We made a good pair."

"Is your housekeeper Anna, the lady who came to college visits with your parents?"

"Yes. Anna started working for my parents before I was born and helped bring me up. She was as excited about me studying in the United States as were my parents. When they passed away she came to my home. I couldn't do without her… Before I forget. What was the name of the class on Polish cooking?"

"I don't remember. I'll look it up online and get the name and phone number when we get to the house. Then can you call and register both of us for the class?" Lily pulled her sunglasses from the collar of her blouse, slipped them on, and pushed them to the bridge of her nose with her index finger. "It's a beautiful day. Not a cloud in the sky."

"Is the name of the program *Cooking with Anika Bartnik* by chance?"

"Yes. How did you know?"

"I took a guess. I know her. Her program comes on after mine. Maybe I can get her to give us some private lessons. We'll see."

"So tell me what do you mean about her program following yours, Rachel? I didn't know you were working."

"Karl is so busy I have a lot of free time. Anyway, she does a live show after me. It's taped, then sent to many stations in Poland."

"What's your program about?"

"I have a television program at the same local station in the town where we have our vacation home. I talk about travel, places one should visit, and the local color and sights of the cities I report on. It forces Karl to take time off, and we do some traveling so I have first-hand info on the places I report on. He reads while I tape my show then we have fun. We make sure we vacation here at Christmas. Neither of us work. The town is beautiful at that time of the year, decorations on all the shops and homes."

"Where are we going, Rachel?"

"We're going to Kazimierz Dolny. A village with cobblestone streets and quaint shops. Its south and about one hundred and forty kilometers from Warsaw or eighty-eight miles, in your lingo. We won't be far from the city limits of Krakow. The climate is mild all year long. It's a beautiful town. There is no rail connection so it's not on every tourist's itinerary. It's on the east side of the Vistula

River, very rural and quiet. It's a great place to vacation if you really want to be in beautiful surroundings."

"It sounds like Eden."

"It is. You can rejuvenate your body and mind. Between WWI and WWII a group of painters of the St. Luke Fellowship came to the village. They started the wave of writers, musicians, and artists coming to live in the area year-round. It's too bad you didn't visit the last week of June for our Music Festival. There were many bands, singers, and music, old and new. They presented music rarely performed today. In August, we have a film and art festival. A lot of actors come to town. You missed that too. I taped both festivals so you can watch them while you're here."

"Next time I'll plan on visiting for one of them. But right now, I can see all the fall colors and the beautiful scenery at this time of the year. Plus, we have a lot of catching up to do."

"We're almost there."

"How long have you owned the house?"

"It belonged to my great-grandmother. They lived in Warsaw during World War II in an apartment, because the Germans commandeered the house. A general took it over because it was near the camps of Auschwitz-Birkenau. The population of the town used to be almost all Jewish. The Germans liquidated 60,000 of them. My great-grandmother was Jewish, but she was married to a Christian who was a Colonel in the German army. The Nazis left the family alone. At the end of the war, the family had to go to court to prove the house belonged to us. It took years. There were still problems until about fourteen or so years ago. Karl's family helped. They have a lot of connections. Even after all these years, there are still a few things to sort out. Things move slowly."

"You are lucky he's in the government."

"We completely redecorated it when we got back. It's really beautiful, built with sandstone and slate on the roof. It backs up against gardens that are in front of a lawn and the Vistula River. A forest is on the other side of the water. It's in a picturesque area." Rachel glanced to her right. "Here we are."

Lily stared at the house. A chill ran up her spine.

CHAPTER TWO

Lily heard the crack of gravel as the tires of Rachel's Fiat drove on the long driveway. A tan stucco house sat in the middle of a large yard. A shoulder high iron fence separated the front yard from the street. Box Wood hedges divided the side yards from the neighbors' yards. Window boxes attached to the bottom of large windows were filled with the fall colors of deep red, orange, and gold chrysanthemums on both the first and second floors. The windows had dark, brown shutters.

Rachel pulled up to the pavement at the side door of the house.

Jumping out of the car, Lily moved to the back as she waited for Rachel to pop open the trunk. When she heard it open, she grabbed her large case and pulled up the handle.

"Okay, I'll take your purse and small case."

Lily listened to the dry leaves on the sidewalk crunch under her feet and wheels of her suitcase as she and her friend walked into the house. As she looked around, she shivered. Her face clouded with uneasiness when she pulled off her sunglasses. A warning voice whispered in her head. "Be careful." A cool breeze made her shiver again. Apprehension coursed through her as she followed Rachel.

"What's wrong?" Rachel asked. "All of a sudden you look pale and you're shivering. Are you cold?"

"No. I don't know what's wrong. I just feel a little strange. I'm sure it's nothing. Don't worry. I'm fine."

"I hope Anna has started fires in the hearths in all the rooms," Rachel said. "We still have so many nice days we haven't turned on the furnace. Fires in the fireplaces seem to warm up the house enough."

Lily forced a smile. *I'm not really cold. It's a shiver of dread.* Bewildered, she didn't share this thought with Rachel.

As her friend pulled on the brass handle of a huge wooden door, it swung open noiselessly on its bronze hinges. "We always enter through this door on the side of the house. We hardly ever use the front door."

Trailing Rachel through the kitchen, her suitcase bounced on the tiles. A huge oak table and chairs with seat cushions covered in a large plaid in shades of rust, red, and gold sat in the middle of the kitchen. The aroma of herbs and chicken wafted from a large pot sitting on one of the burners of an eight-burner stove in front of her. "What do I smell?"

"That's our soup. We're having a vegetable chicken stew with a salad for lunch."

"Yummy. I'm hungry."

"Follow me. I'll show you to your room so you can get settled then we'll eat." Rachel led Lily through the dining room. Another large oak table and chairs sat on an Oriental carpet in front of a fireplace. The cushions of the chairs matched the colors of the drapes. They were covered in blues, from navy to powder. A fire burned in the huge stone fireplace with a hearth also opening into the living room.

Lily glanced at the heavy oak furniture in the living room. Chair covers and drapes were in brocade and velvet. Their colors were burgundy, red, purples, tans, and browns. A mix of Oriental rugs in geometric and floral designs and different sizes covered dark hardwood floors.

Lily smelled leather and saw one wall was covered from floor to ceiling with shelves holding books. Candle holders with candlesticks and family photographs sat on the tables. A variety of oil paintings hung on the walls. A brown leather overstuffed couch and two tan leather chairs sat in front of the fireplace.

Rachel walked from the living room into a spacious entrance way. Following her friend, Lily looked toward the end of the hallway leading from the entry to the back of the house. Her eyes stared through a glass door of the front corridor into gardens filled with fall flowers.

Behind her, a large, narrow oak table with flowers that looked as if they came from the garden sat in its middle. Ahead of her, a curved stone staircase with a smooth, well-polished wooden banister led to the second floor. Terra-cotta urns filled with a variety of light and dark green plants sat on either side of the first step. Lily pushed down the handle of the large suitcase and carried it up.

At the top of stairs, she stared down the long hallway covered with a geometric designed runner in the same colors of the living room. Oil paintings hung on the hall walls. Each one had a light attached to the top frame so that it could be viewed better than it would in the hallway's dim light.

"The master suite is here." Rachel pointed to the room on her right and opened the door.

Lily peeked in. Reds, whites, and blacks were the colors used in her friend's bedroom.

Rachel flicked the switch on the wall next to her room. "This lights up the hall."

"We overlook the front of the house. Your room is the last one on the left. You'll overlook the gardens, river, and woods filled with hundreds of huge, old pine trees. Come on. I can't wait for you to see it," she said as they walked down the hall.

Lily looked up at the lights hanging from the ceiling as they strolled. "You have high ceilings."

"The ceilings are twelve feet." Rachel turned the large brass doorknob and pushed open a heavy, wooden door when she reached the guest room.

Lily stared at the fireplace on her right as she entered. A fire burned, but its warmth didn't completely make the chill that had crept through her earlier disappear.

"Relax for a few minutes then we'll have lunch." Rachel placed Lily's purse and case on the bedside table next to a Tiffany lamp with an off-white and turquoise geometric pattern and an off-white shade. Reaching out, she took her friend's large case. Closing the handle, she picked it up and put it on the bench at the end of the bed.

"There's a bathroom behind that door." Rachel pointed to a door next to a desk.

"Just a minute." Lily walked to the table and reached into the pocket of her suitcase and pulled out her laptop, placing it on the bedside table. "Let me give you the number for the cooking class. Do you have Wi-Fi?"

"Yes." Rachel gave her the code, as she looked around the room. "Can I help you hang your clothes?"

"No. That's okay. I'll do it later." Lily looked at the curtains. "What's behind them?"

Rachel walked to the floor-length, deep turquoise, satin drapes near the bed and pulled them open exposing French doors.

Lily pushed the start button on her computer, waited for it to boot up, then typed in the Wi-Fi code and the show name of the chef she was interested in meeting.

"Here's the number, 002/310-10-00. Want me to write it down?" Lily asked.

"No. I can remember it."

"I'm going to throw some water on my face and rest for a few minutes. Will be down in about forty-five minutes."

"Good. That'll give me time to make the salad and set up lunch. Let me show you something before I go downstairs," Rachel said as she opened the French doors. On the other side of the doors, there was a stone balcony where three comfortable looking steel chairs surrounding a small, stylish steel table with a glass top. "You can enjoy your first cup of coffee of the day, right here. The chairs are very comfortable," she said as she stood in the doorway to the balcony. "If you leave Anna a note before you go to bed for the night with the time you'll awake, she'll bring it up to you."

Lily walked to her friend and gave her a hug. "It's so good to be here."

Rachel returned the hug and smiled. "See you in a little while," she said as she opened the door and closed it quietly behind her.

Lily stared out the French doors. The size of the garden surprised her. It spread the length of the house. Brick paths wound through and surrounded the assortment of flowering shrubs and two bubbling fountains. A river drifted lazily past its banks and the gardens.

A dark cloud filled the sky. A fog lifted from the river. "What?" Lily walked onto the balcony, leaned over the rail, and stared. A group of men and women in ragged striped clothes splashed through the river and finally ran into the woods. They were followed by men in German soldier uniforms and dogs, who seemed confused when they reached the river bank. *Who are they? What's going on?*

Good, they escaped. Her eyes burned as she rubbed them. When she looked into the woods again, the sun began to break through the clouds. The vision was gone. Turning, she rushed into the room, immediately pulling the French doors closed. Lily looked for a lock and a key. Finding neither, she pulled the drapes close.

Slipping out of her clothes, except for her lacy underwear, she threw them on the overstuffed chair in front of the fireplace. It was covered with what appeared to be satin in a dark shade of turquoise. Quickly walking toward the high bed, she moved matching light turquoise pillows to one side of the bed as she thought about what she had seen. Before she slid under the floral duvet, she walked to the balcony doors. Pushing one of the drapes aside, she peered out through the panes to the back grounds of the house.

Lily stared. No one was there. Rays of sunlight sparkled as they bounced off the moving water of the river. She pulled the drapes closed and walked back to the bed. She sat on the side away from the doors and set her smartphone alarm for a half hour.

After a brief scan of the room, she walked to an ornately carved desk and chair sitting under a window looking over the side of the house. These drapes were open. No one was there when she peered out. The desk was next to the bathroom door and near to the large stone fireplace with a wooden mantle and the overstuffed chair. Flames shot from the logs piled on the hearth. The door of the armoire, placed on the far wall was partially open. Satin padded hangers were visible through its half-opened door. She smiled. *Only Rachel would have hangers matching the color scheme of the room. I'll unpack later.*

She sat on the side of the bed, flung her feet up, and slipped her feet under the duvet. She pulled it up to her chin. Shadows played on the walls as the sun lit the room.

The only noise she heard was the water of the river bubbling and splashing along the river bottom.

   Startled, she sat up. Her eyes flew open. The alarm on her smartphone buzzed loudly. She leaned over and grabbed her phone off the bedside table. Pushing the side button, the buzzing stopped. She peered around the room, then stared at the ceiling. *What is happening? What happened on the train last night? What did I see in the river and woods behind the gardens today?* Were these real vision or dreams. She jumped out of bed, ran to the French doors, pulled open the curtains, and looked at the grounds through the glass panes as she had done before her nap. Sun glared over the flagstones of the garden.

   As she watched, the sky darkened and a fog settled over the river. "No…it can't be happening again. One, two…" she counted. There were at least ten men and women in the same loosely fitted, ripped clothes of the others she saw. Her eyes watered as she rubbed them. "They also ran from the river into the woods." She threw open the French doors and darted to the railing. "Hey. Hey. Stop. Wait," she yelled. "I've got to see if they are real people." As they disappeared, she turned quickly, ran back into the bedroom, leaving the French doors open. "I have to talk to Rachel. I have to find out if these people are real."

   Covering the short distance to the bathroom door, she twisted the knob and flung it open. The door handle hit the wall. *Okay, slow down. You'll destroy the wall.* Reaching over, she pulled the door toward her as she checked, running her hand over the wall. *Thank goodness no dent, no damage.* This time she gently pushed on the door so it met the wall with a tap. When her bare feet hit the cold tiles of the bathroom floor, she jumped.

Not taking the time to look around, she threw her underwear on the floor and turned on the hot water faucet of the bathtub. The water wasn't warm when she stuck the toes of her right foot in. *It's not too bad.* She shivered as she climbed over the side of the tub and had to stand in the cold running water. Splashing water on her face, she quickly washed the train trip off. Then soaped the rest of her body and let the water that finally warmed run over her body rinsing it off.

"Just when I'm ready to get out, the water is getting hot." She grabbed a towel from the rack beside the tub and wrapped it around her. "This is pretty…turquoise." A glance around the room. "Leave it to Rachel. The floor tiles, shower curtain, and towels have picked up all the colors in the bedroom."

Rubbing herself dry, she wrapped the towel around her and tucked one end so it wouldn't slide off. Back in the bedroom, she opened her suitcase and pulled out ecru slacks, a lavender, silk blouse, and lavender lacy underwear. As she dressed, sun filled the room. Glancing out beyond the balcony, she saw that no one wandered through the grounds. Only a gardener pulled weeds in a bed of flowers. Lily dug into her case, pulling out her makeup and brush. Hunting at the bottom, she found a lavender ribbon hidden under the rest of her clothes and pulled it out.

She walked quickly to the bathroom, hung her towel that she had let drop on the floor, and flicked on the light over the sink. After applying mascara and eyebrow darkener, she ran a brush through her hair and tied it with the ribbon at her neck. Hopping from foot to foot, she slipped on low-heeled, ecru shoes as she closed the French doors and room door. The hallway was empty as she ran to the stairs leading to the first floor.

"Rachel. Rachel, where are you?" Lily called out when her feet hit the large tiles of the entranceway.

"I'm in the kitchen fixing the salad. If you're at the bottom of the staircase, turn left and walk to the end of the hallway as if you're going into the garden. The kitchen is the last room on your right. It's just before the door to the gardens."

"The soup still smells wonderful."

"The salad is small but has lots of vegetables. We won't eat dinner until Karl gets here at about eight. He called and said he was looking forward to seeing you and would come tonight and go back to the city with us for the concert, then come back on the weekend."

"Oh good, it will be great to see him."

"You look lovely in lavender. It goes well with your strawberry blond hair and green eyes."

"Thanks. Rachel, I have to tell you something." Furrows formed in her brow.

"Okay, sit. We can talk while we eat," Rachel said as she placed a bowl of soup on the table in front of her friend. "Just a minute. Don't start yet." Pulling on the refrigerator handle, she opened it, leaned down, and produced a bottle from the bottom shelf. When she stood, she held up a long neck, glass bottle. "Some white wine?"

"I would love a glass, but maybe I shouldn't. Let me tell you what's been happening to me."

"Nonsense. Nothing can be that bad. I know the French have wine with every meal except breakfast. We Pols have vodka, but I thought you would prefer wine." Rachel peeled off the paper from the top of the bottle then twisted the cork up and out with an opener from the shelf next to her.

"Yes. Wine please." Lily laughed as she picked up some soup on her spoon and tasted it. "This is great. You've learned how to cook."

"I can't take the credit. Anna made it." Rachel filled two wine glasses.

"Mm…" Lily smelled its bouquet. "A nice Chablis."

Sitting Lily's glass in front of her, she filled two small plates with salad. "The dressing is lite, just olive oil and lemon juice. Do you want some bread?"

"No thanks. Soup and salad are enough."

"Now tell me, what is bothering you?" she asked as she sat and took a sip of her wine.

"Well, on the trip here I had a dream. Or at least I thought it was a dream."

"Yes."

"When I first got on the train, I finished my column and emailed it to my editor and then emailed you. Then I fell asleep. A noise woke me up. The train had changed. I was on an old train, one from the nineteen thirties or forties. I got out of bed and threw open my window and stuck my head out. I saw the smoke pouring from the engine. It passed my compartment window. I didn't recognize where I was." She smiled. "While I was staring out the window to see if I could see something in my surroundings that was familiar to me, I heard a sharp knock on my door. A man dressed in a brown shirt and trousers and Jackboots was standing outside my compartment. He had a red armband with a black swastika in a white circle like the Nazis wore during World War II." Lily sighed.

"When I slid open the door, he demanded my papers. I didn't know what he meant and didn't know what to do. He kept demanding my papers. Finally, I had it and handed him my passport. That seemed to satisfy him. Rachel, he was so real." Taking a deep breath, she took a sip of wine. "It must have been a dream." She smiled.

"There's more. When you left my room, I went out on the balcony. I could have sworn I saw a group of men and women running through the river behind the gardens. They ran into the forest. They were being chased by Nazi soldiers and dogs."

Rachel took a bite of her salad and chewed… "Lily you weren't dreaming. I've seen them also."

"Do you see them often?"

"No. Not now. At first, when I was young I did. I must tell you they scared me. They still appear once in a while. Now, I just try not to let them bother me. I tuck them in the back of my mind. I decided they are ghosts from World War Two who haven't passed over yet. They haven't been able to find peace. Maybe they have stayed here to teach us a lesson about what can happen if we let someone like Hitler get into power."

"You told me the Nazis took your house because it was close to the camps."

"I did. Remember I told you my great-grandmother was Jewish but was safe because of my great-grandfather's connections. I didn't tell you that after a while they shared the house with the officer who was single and didn't need all the space. My great-grandparents also spent time in an apartment in Warsaw during the war." She took some soup.

"Even though my great-grandfather was a soldier, he didn't agree with the Nazis and used to help hide some of the Jews right under the Nazi's noses and helped them escape. My great-grandparents were very careful. They never got caught."

"How did the Nazis get away with what happened?"

"Even though there were rumors of the horrors happening in the camps, most of the people didn't want to know or couldn't believe the rumors they heard could possibly be true."

"Were there any escapes?"

"Many were successful and some not. Most dug tunnels or left work details. One of the ones I heard about was unbelievable. Let me tell you about it."

"I'm all ears." Lily waited for Rachel to continue.

"One night a group of men made up their minds they were going to find out exactly what was going on in Auschwitz. They had false papers made and allowed themselves to be taken in on a roundup. Before they were captured, they set up ways to get messages out of the camp. They were told by the prisoners what was truly going on." Rachel sighed. "After they got out a lot of messages, they decided it was time to escape. They overtook a group of guards and killed them. After they dressed in their uniforms, they dressed the guards in their clothes and buried them behind the barracks. They overtook Heinrich Himmler's driver, tied him up, and stole his jeep. They drove out of the camp to a farmer's house. He gave them clothes. They buried the uniforms and dumped the jeep in the river."

"What happened to them then?"

"The men told everyone what was happening, what actually went on in the camps. They went all over Poland, telling their story. The people finally believed what the men told them especially when their reports were read. The underground newspapers published their story. That's when more and more Pols became active in the underground and resistance becoming more active in defeating the Germans. The resistance steadily grew with both men and women."

"I'm beginning to think I wasn't dreaming, but I did go back in that time."

"You were like that in college. Sometimes it was eerie, Lily."

"I know. My sister, Violet, is better at conjuring up past times than I am. She really has the "Sight" as the Irish called it. I never told anyone I had it too because it didn't happen very often to me. At a young age, I especially hid it when I realized people thought Violet was weird. I kept the incidents of "The sight," to myself so they wouldn't say that about me."

"I always thought your sister was nice, the few times I met her."

"Thanks. Violet was estranged from the family for about fifteen years. Now we're all friends."

"Why?"

"It's a long and bitter story. Her twin Daisy always made trouble and stole her boyfriend. It was very nasty. It's all settled now. We're one big happy family."

"Good. Let's get some exercise. We can walk into the village. I need some bread for tonight's dinner, some pastries for dessert, and breakfast rolls."

"Sounds good. I need to work up an appetite for dinner. Lunch filled me." Taking her last sip of wine, Lily looked up when she heard footsteps.

"Anna. Remember my best friend when I was in school in the United States? Lily this is Anna, the lady I couldn't do without."

Lily watched her stand with her hands on her ample hips. Her hair pulled back in a bun at the base of her neck had grayed. A flowered apron was tied at her waist and hung over a long sleeve, calf-length navy dress. Her sleeves were pushed toward her elbows, and she wore low-heeled shoes with laces tied just below her ankles. Beads of perspiration formed on her forehead. She brushed them away with the large white handkerchief she pulled from the pocket of her apron.

"I remember meeting you at graduation. It's good to see you." Lily smiled as she grabbed Anna's free hand. She stared at the wrist of the housekeeper's right hand. *I never remembered a tattoo of numbers. Must have worn long sleeves when I met her.* Lily dropped her arms, averted her eyes away from Anna's wrist, and put her arms around her giving her a hug.

"It's so nice to see you. I'm glad you are visiting. Rachel never stopped talking about you since she found out you were going to visit." Anna smiled. "How is your mother?"

"Fine. After a bad second marriage, she decided she would spend her life visiting her grandchildren and children. I suspect she'll be coming to France one of these days to visit me."

"Anna, it's such a beautiful sunny day, we're going to walk into the village. Don't worry about the mess in the kitchen. I'll clean it up when we get back."

"Go. It will only take me a few minutes." Anna waved them out of the kitchen with the back of her hand.

"The soup was wonderful," Lily shouted as she slipped on her sunglasses and started down the side steps to the driveway.

"I'm sorry I should have asked about your mother. I was so busy catching up on your dreams and work I forgot," Rachel said.

"Don't worry about it. I think you only met her once. Now tell me all about what's been going on with you." Lily requested as she and Rachel walked.

"Well, Karl is Jewish. I think you knew that."

Lily nodded.

"Most of his family were exterminated by the German soldiers during World War II. Many were shot or died of disease or gassed in the camps. We've been very active in Holocaust survivor's groups."

"How horrible. Does he ever talk about what went on or how he feels?"

"Yes. Sometimes he mentions how our children will never get to know his side of the family and how all their treasures were lost. He is sad the children, when we have them, will have no memory of their heritage. I always tell him we'll make our own family history." She smiled, but a tear ran down her cheek.

"I saw you notice Anna's wrist. Her dresses usually have long sleeves. Being Jewish, she was taken prisoner when she was a young child. Nuns at the convent in Warsaw smuggled her out of the Ghetto and hid her for a while in their orphanage. Relatives of our family took her in when the orphanage became overcrowded and hid her in the attic of their house in Warsaw. Toward the end of the war in 1945, the Germans found her. At five years old, the soldiers captured her and dragged her into a truck. They drove her and others onto a cattle car of a train. It took her to Auschwitz. Almost crushed in the train car because they stuffed so many people in they couldn't sit down and could barely stand up, she told me she made the trip."

"Did she tell you why they were found?"

"It must have been some who needed food or favors who turned them in."

"What happened to the family?"

"The family who hid her was shot to death right in front of her eyes."

"It must have been horrible for such a small child. It must have been so frightening."

"When she got to the camp, she was in a large room with other women, young and old. Hiding under the bunk in the barracks or under some of the women where she lived for several months saved her when the guards came to lead them to the gas chamber." Rachel sighed. "When she was finally caught and was about to be walked into the showers, this was what the Germans called the gas chambers, the American soldiers attacked the camp and captured the guards. They found her hiding under a bunk."

"Didn't any of the prisoners who knew about the gas chamber tell the others?"

"No. They were afraid. Those who knew what was going on would be shot as well as the prisoners they told if the soldiers found out they revealed what was happening. There were spies in the barracks who reported these people to the soldiers. The only thing those who knew could do was hide in the barracks and hope they wouldn't be found. Some hid under dead bodies of prisoners who died from disease or hunger."

"Are we near town?" Lily asked, beginning to feel horrible with the way the conversation was going.

"Yup. See the brick wall? We turn left there. It's Main Street." Rachel pointed to the wall and the street a few feet in front of them. She glanced at Lily. "I know it's hard to hear about the war, but we should never forget what happened."

"You're right, but I'm beginning to feel depressed," Lily said as she turned left. "I see the bakery sign. It's just a few steps away." Lily looked down the main road of the village.

"We're here," Rachel said as they turned the corner to the Main Street. "See what I mean? It's a quaint village with narrow cobblestone streets and artistic signs over the doors of the food shops and boutiques. Artists set up their easels on the street and the corners of the restaurant patios on nice days."

CHAPTER THREE

Lily stared through the window of the bakery at the glass cases with shelves of baked goods. Removing her sunglasses, she hooked them into the neck of her blouse.

"Good afternoon, Elka," Rachel said as she pulled open the door of the bake shop." This is my friend from the United States, Lily. Lives in Paris now and is visiting me for a while. I want to introduce her to some of your wonderful pastries." Rachel smiled at her friend.

"Hi, Lily. Welcome to our village."

"Hello, Elka. Everything smells and looks so good." Lily smiled.

"What do you need today?" Elka smiled.

"I walk here and visit the bakery almost every day when I'm staying in the village." Rachel laughed. "I'll take a loaf of the rye. You'll like it, Lily. It's made with buttermilk and has a slightly tangy taste. What looks good to you in the sweets department?" Rachel watched her friend scanning the shelves with the sweets.

Lily smiled. "I don't know what to select."

"Don't worry. We'll come back in again soon. You can select different ones. You'll be here long enough to enjoy many of the sweets."

Lily pointed to three of the desserts in front of her.

"We'll have three Parskis. You'll like them they're like doughnuts and are filled with preserves. Three Serniks, they are cheesecake, and three poppy seed cakes. The poppy seed cakes have some liqueur in them. I think its rum," Rachel said. "Am I right?"

"You're right. I just took them out of the oven," Elka said. "That's why the aroma is so strong."

"Good, we'll have them for dessert tonight. They are Karl's favorite."

Lily eyes fix on the shelf to her left.

"Did you just finish baking those too?" Rachel pointed to the pastry Lily stared at.

"Yes."

"Okay, Elka, give us three pancakes, please."

"They look so good. What are they stuffed with?" Lily smiled.

"Apples and spices. When they cool, I dust them with powdered sugar." She smiled.

"That should be enough to last us until Wednesday." Rachel laughed. "I forgot how much you loved sweets." After the owner slipped her purchases into bags, she dug some Zloty from her pocket and paid. "Thank you." Waving at the owner, she pushed open the bakery door.

"I guess we should be starting back. We're going that way." She stood on the steps of the store and turned, pointing to the wall at the end of the street. "I have some things to do at home for my TV program before Karl gets here."

"Would you mind if I stayed in town for a while? I would like to look in some of the boutiques and galleries. If you don't need help carrying the bags of baked goodies."

"No. Do you know your way back?"

"I think so. But, I wasn't really paying much attention when we walked into town. I was looking at the scenery and listening to your story about Anna."

"Walk to the end of the street." Rachel pointed to her left again." Take a right at the brick wall. Follow the road until you see our house. The river will always be on your right. See you in a little while. But before you come home go to the market square. In the center, there's a wooden well. You can see it from here. See it?" Pointing to her right, she smiled. "They say if you throw in a coin and make a wish it will come true. There are lots of great shops looking out on the square too."

Lily waved as she turned and walked toward the town square. As she stopped and stood in front of an art gallery, she looked at the paintings by Polish artists in the window. After several minutes a fog drifted in from the Vistula River.

October 1939

The day became dark and damp. Just as she was about to enter the gallery, she heard the pounding of heavy boots on the cobblestone street and the rumbling of moving vehicles. The fog cleared. She peered up the street. Disoriented, she looked around. People walking on the street scattered into buildings. A large group of German soldiers marched in front of thirty tons of steel tanks. Large trucks, with canvas-covered backs that flapped in the breeze, brought up the rear. They broadcast a speech by Hitler through large speakers on the roofs of the trucks as they headed toward her. Looking around, she nervously bit her lip. A soft gasp escaped her. Icy fear twisted around her heart as it jumped in her chest. A shiver ran through her. A cold knot formed in her stomach. *Where should I go? Where can I hide?*

From the corner of her eye, she saw a tall figure step from the shadows. When she felt one of his arms envelop her and the other grip her wrist, she was confused. When he pulled her into the alley next to the gallery, she was bewildered. Lifting her head, she stared into the face of a man bronzed by the wind and sun with thick, black hair tapering neatly at his collar. A lock fell a little forward onto his forehead. Her mind clouded with uneasiness as a shock ran through. Her eyes met his deep brown ones.

He stared. "Are you all right. The color has drained from your face. You're not going to faint are you?" he asked.

She took a deep breath and swallowed with difficulty, trying to manage a feeble answer. Finally, she found her voice. "I'm okay. Just a bit shaken with what was coming toward us." Her breath was shallow and came in quick gasps. "I don't know where to hide."

"Don't be scared. Play along with me."

As the din of the soldiers marching got closer, he put his index finger to his lips, to silence her. When the first line of men reached the alley, she felt him pull her into his arms, crushing her to him. "Just pretend we're a couple," he whispered into her ear.

She stood with him not looking at the soldiers. After a few minutes, she realized the echo of boots on the cobblestones and the roar of engines had diminished. The convoy had passed the alley. They were no longer in danger. When she felt his grip on her arms loosen, she flattened her palms against his chest and pushed back. Her body stiffened as she crossed her arms over her chest and studied him.

His massive shoulders filled his black leather jacket. A beautifully proportioned body strained against his white t-shirt and black trousers. He looked tough and lean. His lips parted when he smiled, displaying a dazzling set of white teeth. Her pulse skittered. Finally, she was able to speak. "Why…? Why did you do that?" Her lips burned.

"I knew you weren't from here. I've never seen you in the village. A beautiful woman would attract their attention. I figured if the SS thought we were lovers, sneaking a kiss, they wouldn't stop and bother us. I didn't want them to interrogate you." He scrutinized her. "The SS soldiers have been known to pull people into their trucks and take them in for questioning or to the camps. It depends on their mood. Sometimes the people are never seen again. They have already begun a roundup of people they look on as undesirables."

"Well, you're right about that. I know I would never be able to stand up to the questioning of Hitler's secret police." Lily peeked around the corner of the building. "You're right. Look!" Sticking out her hand, she grabbed his, pulling him next to her. "A group of soldiers has broken rank. They are dragging two men to their truck at the end of the convoy. They're being shoved into the back." When the flap of canvas covering the opening at the back of the truck flew open, she saw a group of men and women wearing yellow arm bands imprinted with the Star of David huddled together in the truck bed.

"The roundups are becoming more frequent. It gets worse with each day. You better get to wherever you are staying. They could turn around and come back." He raised his hand and pushed a lock of her hair that had escaped her ribbon behind her ear. He smiled.

The warmth of his smile echoed in his voice while he spoke and studied her. A warmth crept from her chest to her cheeks. "Thanks for saving me. I have to leave."

"Wait!" He reached for her arm, holding it gently. Where are you staying?" He stared into her green eyes.

"I'm from France and staying just up the road with my friend Rachel Dabrowsky and her husband. She's doing some work for…" She couldn't say work for her TV program. If she was indeed in 1940, very few local people had televisions. Those who did weren't looking at travel shows. "I decided to walk around the town." Turning, she began to walk away, not wanting to get into more conversation.

"I'm French also. Where do you live in France?"

"I'm from the United States. Just moved to a small apartment on the Left Bank of the Seine River in Paris." She stopped.

With a raised hand to shelter her eyes, she looked down the street at the soldiers. "I have to go." A wave of apprehension swept through her. "Some of the soldiers have left the group and are wandering around. I don't have my passport with me. I'd better get going. Thank you very much for helping me."

"Okay. Hope I see you again. I'm Pierre Girard."

"Lily O'Malley," she yelled over her shoulder as she ran toward the brick wall, but he had disappeared. Some of the soldiers were walking in her direction.

When she looked again, the soldiers were entering one of the shops. After a quick turn right at the end of the street and the start of the brick wall, Lily felt safe. Picking some wildflowers as she walked, she heard a voice calling her. When she looked up, Rachel was waving as she ran toward her.

"Lily. Stop. Stay away."

Lily didn't move. "What's going on?" she asked when her friend reached her.

"The Nazis are here. I saw them coming and managed to get out of the house before they broke in. Come on. We have to hide in the woods until we can figure out what to do."

"What about your great-grandparents?"

"They must be at the apartment in town."

"How are we going to get across the river?" Lily asked.

Rachel dragged her up the driveway behind the hedges on the neighbor's side. At the back side of her property, she pushed through the hedges and pulled her into a shed. "There are two canoes in this outbuilding. We'll each take one. Let's hope we can get across the river before they see us."

Rachel threw open the door of the shed and ran to the back wall of the building. "Help me get them off the hooks."

Brushing off several spiders and their webs, Lily helped pull them off the wall hooks. She grabbed one end and watched Rachel pick up the other. She walked backward toward the door and pulled it out of the shed to the river bank. Lily and her friend ran back to the shed. She grabbed one end of the second canoe and with Rachel at the other end they pulled it out of the shed. Finally, each canoe sat behind the shed at the river bank.

"Wait, we need paddles." Rachel glanced around when they reached the river bank. "Where did I put them? Oh yea, under the workbench." The front end of her canoe dropped into the edge of the river. She ran back into the shed. Throwing back the tarp, she grabbed the paddles.

"One for each canoe."

Lily heard a thump as Rachel dropped a paddle in each boat.

"I'm going to peek around the other side of the building and see if anyone is there." She pointed to her right. "Where we're standing now, the back of the shed is hidden. The chances of anyone seeing us enter the river from the house is probably nil unless they are on the second floor. But they can see us when we're on the river." Rachel frowned.

Lily slipped off her shoes, tossed them in the bottom of the boat, and rolled up her slacks. "Rachel get into your canoe. I'll push you into the water." Taking a deep breath made Lily feel better.

"The garden is empty, but let's hope no one is looking out the windows."

Rachel pushed her canoe paddle into the water and propelled her boat.

Lily watched her friend raise her paddle and wave. "Start paddling fast. I'll catch up." She slipped her canoe into the river and followed.

"What are we going to do?" Rachel whined, looking back at Lily.

"Let me think. Wait. We're almost to the other side. When we hit the shore, hop out and pull the boat up onto the bank." When she felt the canoe hit the land, she slid her shoes on, crept to the front, and jumped out. "Come on, let's get it into the woods. I see a clump of bushes just ahead. Pick up the front of your boat. We'll drag them behind the bushes and hide them there. Hurry."

Just as they finished hiding the canoes, Lily saw the figure of a man in a uniform on the other side of the river. He left the house by the garden door.

"Duck down. He's walking into the garden. Looks like an officer. He'll be there for a while."

"How do you know?"

"He's smoking." Lily sat down behind the bushes and leaned against a pine tree. Deep breathing did no good when she tried to relax. Fear knotted inside her. Getting to her knees, she peeked around the shrubs. She put her index finger to her lips. "Don't talk. He's walking toward the river bank and other soldiers have joined him," she whispered.

A flicker of apprehension coursed through her. "Oh good, someone must have called him." When she watched him throw his cigarette into the water, her fear eased. "He's going back into the house. Okay, the door is shut. The others have walked toward the front of the house. Let's get further into the trees and then we can decide what we're going to do." Her slacks felt wet. A critical eye glanced down at them. *They're filthy. They're my favorite. I love them. Oh well, Rachel will help me get some new ones if we ever get back to 2014.*

There was silence except for the crunching of leaves under their feet as they walked.

"Do you hear that?" Lily asked.

"No."

"We're not the only ones crunching leaves and cracking twigs under our feet. Someone is behind us. I hope they aren't following us." Lily came to an abrupt stop. Finding it impossible to steady her erratic pulse or a momentary panic attack, she took a deep breath. Her heart jumped in her chest. Her deep breath cut off as she watched soldiers suddenly appear on the bank of the river across from where the canoes were hidden. A sense of strength came to her and her fear lessened.

"They don't seem to be looking at the woods." She held up her hand and stared at Rachel. "But, I hear footsteps. It isn't the soldiers they're still on the bank. Have you seen anyone cross the river?" A shadow of alarm touched her face.

"No. Well, I'm not sure. I'm sorry I haven't been paying attention. I don't see any boats in the water or on the bank."

"Duck down behind the bushes." Lily pushed her friend to the clump of bushes on their left. Fear knotted inside her stomach as she bent down. She peeked through the branches. Her body stiffened in shock. A soft gasp escaped her lips as she stared up into the faces of men and women, some looking like teenagers. They dressed in combat jackets, trousers, and boots. They had red armbands on their arms. Their heads were covered with berets. Usually not at a loss for words, she stood silently in surprise, her heart pounding.

The leader hesitated, measuring her for a minute as the group pointed their guns at her. "Put your hands up and walk."

Lily started to raise her hands, then dropped them to her sides, sliding them into the pockets of her slacks as she came to an abrupt stop. As she stared at the group, her heart jumped in her chest when she stared at the man who came up behind them. There was a sign of recognition as she stared into his eyes. "It's you." She gazed up into dark brown eyes and into the face of the man she had met earlier in town and smiled.

"It is okay, Rachel. I don't know these people, but I met this man in the village after you left." Her finger pointed to the man she had played lovers with. "He helped me in town so the German soldiers wouldn't capture and question me." Even though she was calmer than she had been in town, she still felt a warmth crept from her chest to her cheeks as she remembered what had happened. *Don't think anything but friendship. Remember I'm from a different time.*

"It's all right." He motioned for the group to put down their guns.

"Why are you in the woods?" he asked looking at her quizzically.

"We have to stay away from the house. The Germans have taken it over." Rachel stared at the group.

Lily turned toward the house. The German general had appeared again and was standing in the gardens. A wave of apprehension made her heart jump in her chest. A panic like she'd never known before welled in her throat, as she watched him point toward the woods, deep furrows etched her forehead. Panic choked back a cry of fright.

"When I left you in the village and started home, my friend...Oh, this is Rachel. Rachel, Pierre. You disappeared before I could tell you my name. I'm Lily."

He nodded. "Hello, Lily."

"This is the only place we could go. Rachel caught me before I turned into the driveway and told me what happened at the house. The soldiers must be part of the group we saw in the village."

"I'm not sure they are the same. German troops are all over the countryside. But, don't worry ladies. They can't see us. We are well hidden." He studied Lily thoughtfully for a moment. A muscle flicked in his tightened jaw as he clamped his back teeth together. "You'll have to come with us…I hope you can keep up." He sighed.

He probably thinks two more people, and women at that, are not what he needs. I'm sure he believes it's going to make it more difficult for him and his group to avoid the Germans. We'll prove him wrong. "Come on Rachel." She grabbed Rachel's hand.

Lily looked over her shoulder, watching two soldiers leaving by the rear door of the house. They marched the housekeeper and gardener to a truck that backed into the yard. Icy fear twisted around her heart and her chest felt as if it would burst when she saw them shoved into the back. "Who are those people?" she whispered to Rachel.

"They're the help. My great-grandmother always hired poor Jews from the Ghetto," Rachel murmured.

"When the people from the house were forced into the back of the transport and the flap was pulled back I saw the people sitting on the floor. It looked as if there were children in the group. They are wearing yellow armbands with a black Star of David." She squinted against the sun and stared. "Oh no. I was right, they are children." Lily breathed in shallow, quick gasps. The flap blew open. Her hands clenched until her nails entered her palm so she wouldn't scream.

"Why are you in the woods?" Pierre asked.

"We're trying to hide until the soldiers go to the camps to hear Hitler's speech. Then we can get back into the house and get some clothes and food." Uncertainty crept into her expression as she spoke to Pierre. "Why are you here?"

He stood motionless. His face set, mouth clamped, and fixed eyes. His brows drew together. For a moment she was able to feel his intent stare. Then she noticed he seemed to relax suddenly. She wasn't able to stop staring at his massive shoulders and slim hips. He was full of virility, holding his head high with pride. His profile was strong and regal. A shadow of a dark beard covered his cheeks and chin. His white t-shirt had been replaced by a black, wool turtleneck sweater.

"What?" He was answering her question and she hadn't been listening. Her thoughts were still with the people in the truck.

"I'm leading this group of Polish Partisans. We have hideouts not only in town but also here in the woods." He smiled. "You can come with us."

"We'll be fine." She turned and started to walk away from him. Lily's heart jumped when his hand gripped her arm and pulled her toward him. The wool of his sweater rubbed against her arm.

"Don't be silly. You need our help. You have no place to go." He stared at Lily.

"Lily, don't be stubborn. He's right, we need his help. We don't know where we're going," Rachel said. "Please, Lily. We should go with them."

"You're right, of course." Lily tried not to meet her friends gaze. "Okay, what's your plan?"

"There's another broadcast by Hitler tomorrow. All the soldiers will leave for Auschwitz to listen again. He speaks to his troops a couple of days then waits for a few days before he speaks again. When they leave, we'll get into the house and you can get what you need." He ground his words between his teeth. "Come on, ladies." His hands were shoved in his pockets and shoulders hunched forward as he stood. The men and women with him stayed behind Lily and Rachel, watching and listening as they waited for Pierre's next move. Once in a while, they whispered among themselves.

"Why are you with the Partisans?"

His expression grew serious. "I'm with the diplomatic core in France and assigned to the French Embassy here in Poland. The resistance members needed training. I'm here for that. They also need help in radio operation, bomb making, and a host of other sabotage tricks." His face closed. "Quiet." He held up his hand to silence the group and listened for a few minutes. "I thought I heard someone, but I don't see anyone. It's okay, it must have been an animal," he said looking around. "If the Poles are going to defeat the Germans, they have to target the rail infrastructure, disrupt the Germans transport and communication by cutting phone lines, making bombs, and the tricks of acting as couriers. The Polish must destroy the German troops using the railroads, bridges, and supply depots near transportation hubs like Warsaw, Lublin, Krakow, and other cities." As he spoke, his eyes never stopped searching his surroundings.

"Bend down," he whispered.

Lily looked behind her and quickly knelt behind the bush next to her.

Two soldiers on the other side of the river talked as they walked toward the river bank and them. A flicker of apprehension coursed through her. Even though they were across the river, bullets from their guns could reach them.

Suddenly the soldiers stopped.

Lily heard a call from the general as he came through the back door. He threw his cigarette in front of him. Twisting the toe of his Jackboot, he ground it out. A group of soldiers following a truck turned and jogged in the general's direction. A sigh of relief escaped her lips.

"The general looks as if he's giving them orders."

"We need to get further into the woods," Pierre said. "Then we can rest."

"Come on," Lily whispered as she grabbed Rachel's hand, pulling her behind her.

Over her shoulder, she saw the soldiers jump into the truck as it started to drive out of the yard. The general stood and watched them.

Lily leaned on Rachel as they slept. Her body was supported by a towering pine away from the group of Partisans. Awaking when the sunlight broke through the tree's branches, a chill ran up her back. There was still had a feeling of fatigue even though she realized she was in the same position she had been in when she fell asleep. Running her fingers through her hair, she tried to smooth some of the wayward strands. Hunting through her pockets for a rubber band was of no use. Her pockets were empty. *I wish I had a toothbrush. My mouth feels as if it is filled with cotton. How did I get in such a mess?*

Lily could feel her long hair that hung loosely, blow across her face in the soft breeze. *Where is a rubber band? I usually have one.*

"Rachel, you know your great-grandmother won't know you are her great-grandchild."

"Yes, it's going to be strange seeing her as a young woman."

Lily watched Pierre. Even though his expression was immobile and solemn he was aware of everything going on around the group. His eyes always watched.

His glance sharpened. He studied her intently. "What are you two whispering about?"

"We were discussing that it won't be too much longer before the Germans will be gone and the house will be empty," Lily said.

His brown eyes studied her thoughtfully for a moment. "Are you sure the house will be vacant?"

"Like you, I heard about Hitler's broadcast in town. The soldiers wouldn't be allowed to miss it. I'm sure they'll be gone by noon. We can get in and steal some food," Lily spoke in a suffocated whisper. There was stillness in the woods, except for the chirping of the birds. When she finished speaking another group of soldiers arrived.

This group of soldiers stood in the back garden of the house and watched a truck pull into the yard. This time soldiers ran from the house carrying long guns in their arms. They handed them out to the group standing in the garden, pulled back the canvas of the truck and piled into the empty back. One of the soldiers didn't follow. He disappeared around the side of the house. Within minutes he backed a jeep into the yard. Jumping out, he opened the passenger door for the general who walked from the garden door. The general sat in the passenger seat. The driver slammed the door, ran around the jeep and slid into his seat. He revved the motor and pulled into the driveway, following the truck as it pulled away. Within a few minutes, they were gone.

"Wait a few minutes to make sure they're all gone," he whispered. It wasn't long before he spoke again. "Okay, come on, let's get in and out of the house as quickly as possible," Pierre called to his group.

Lily and the others ran and pulled the boats from the bushes. They all crowded into the canoes. After crossing the river, they jumped out and pulled the boats well up on the shore, and ran to the back door. The group waited while Rachel turned the knob of the door leading from the garden.

"It's locked…" She jiggled the knob. "And I don't have the key."

"Let me go try the front and side door. I'll come back here through the house or back if they're not locked."

Rachel called over her shoulder as she began to run to the side of the house.

A few seconds later she returned. "They're locked too."

"Okay. I'll take care of the door," Pierre said.

They waited while he reached into his pocket and picked the lock of the garden door.

Lily looked around when the door flew open. Without asking her friend, she pointed to her left. "The kitchen is that way." She looked around as they ran into the kitchen. It didn't quite look the same as it did when she arrived.

The group began to pull bread from the pantry and cheese and meats from the refrigerator. Throwing them into the canvas bags, Rachel spied and pulled from a shelf near the stove. "When they're filled I'll find more," she whispered.

Lily stared at the stove. It had two burners. The refrigerator looked like one from the 1940s. The top compartment was the freezer. There was a huge block of ice sitting in the middle of the space. Meat and cheese leaned against the ice. *It's nice to see how much the house has been updated.*

"Wait." When she tried to say more, her voice wavered. Her face clouded with uneasiness.

CHAPTER FOUR

"Do you hear that?" she whispered to the group.

"What?" Pierre asked.

"Footsteps." Lily pointed to her left. Tip-toeing to the door next to the food cooler. "Where does this door go?"

"To the basement," Rachel answered.

Lily threw open the door. An old woman and a young girl stood on the top step of a staircase. She stared passed them into a dark basement. It was dark behind them. She wasn't able to see anything.

"Please, don't hurt us," the old woman cried out.

"We won't. I promise. What are you doing here?" Lily asked as she smiled and put her arm around the woman's shoulder.

"Mrs. Wise hides us in the cellar. She comes into the house every few days to bring us food. Mrs. Wise and her husband stay when the soldiers are gone. They help us. They're very smart. The Germans never find out. I'm Gilda and this is my granddaughter Anna. We're Jewish. Mrs. Wise is waiting for a place to open up on the escape trail.

We're going to be moved to another home. To a safer place and a place where the people who are being smuggled out of Poland are hidden before they take the trip. When we heard your voices we thought you were the people coming to move us. We've been hiding in the basement since the Germans came yesterday. They took the household help, but didn't find us."

Lily stared at Anna. *If she only knew what was in store for her.*

"Do you know who is coming for you?" Pierre asked.

The old woman nodded. "A nun and priest from the convent in the village. The Germans are all at Auschwitz for the broadcast, so the resistance workers can move around. I'm sure they will come for us soon."

"Go back to you hiding place until they come." He stared at his Partisans, who had each filled a canvas bag and began to pull more sacks from their jacket pockets and started to fill them. One of the Partisans watched out the kitchen window for a car coming up the street.

"We're leaving in a minute. Give a couple of bags to this woman." Pierre said. "Quick. We have to get out of here," he said to his men and women. "We've been here long enough."

"Where are you hiding?" Lily asked Gilda.

"We are in a secret room in the basement. Mrs. Wise's husband doesn't even know about the room. It's behind the shelves lined with canned goods. Mrs. Wise has helped many."

Lily heard the sound of a car nearing the house. A warning voice whispered in her head. "Get back to your hiding place, quick." Lily glanced out of the window as she patted Anna on the head.

"Okay." Grabbing a couple of bags containing bread and a large piece of cheese from the Partisans, she handed them to Gilda. "All right, it's okay. The car didn't stop. It kept going."

"But go. Hurry. Get into the room. We've been here long enough." The light from the kitchen helped her see on her way to the basement. Following them down the stairs, she stood with a worried expression on her face as she watched Gilda pull the carpet away from the door and pushed a button inside the bottom shelf. Lily watched the door slowly scrape across the basement floor as it opened.

Lily stood in the doorway and peered into the room. It was too dark for her to see what it looked like. "What is your room like?"

"It has a table, chairs, and cots with blankets and pillows. There are candles so we can have light. It's not like our homes, but thousands of times better than the Ghetto."

Gilda waved and smiled as she pulled the carpet toward her, hiding the scrape on the floor, and quickly dropped it before the door closed.

Lily took the basement stairs two at a time as she ran back to the kitchen, she peered out of the window. "The road is empty. It's safe for now."

"We better get out of here," Pierre called to his group. "The next car that comes up the driveway might be the new inhabitants."

"Wait a moment, I need to run upstairs and get some clothes," Lily flung the words over her shoulders as she ran through the rooms to the stairs leading to the rooms above her. "I'll get some for you, Rachel."

Rachel called to her friend as she ran from the kitchen. "Lily, remember?"

Not hearing, Lily ran to the stairs and rushed to her room.

She threw open the door to the bedroom Rachel had given her. The only clothes she saw were German army uniforms. They were neatly pressed and hanging in the armoire. As she pressed both hands over her eyes, they fill with tears of frustration. *Of course, my clothes aren't here. I'm in 1940.*

Down the stairs and back to the kitchen she thought about what she would say when everyone noticed she had no clothes in her hand. Staring at Rachel she put her index finger to her closed lips.

"Let's go." Running to the door, she threw it open. "Rachel, I'll tell you about it later."

"You don't have to. I know. I remember."

"Ouch." She whispered as she tripped over a chair next to the back door.

Pierre caught her before she fell.

Stopping, she rubbed her leg.

"Let me see." Pierre bent down and looked at her shin. "It's okay. No broken skin. However, you may have a bruise."

"Where's the clothes?" He stared at her empty hands.

"I can't find anything appropriate."

"All right. Never mind, ladies, you can borrow something from us. Probably from one of the teenage boys. You both look about their size."

"Boys look in your packs when we get back to the woods for some clothes for these ladies," he called as they ran to the canoes.

They pushed the boats into the water, crowded into them, and paddled to the opposite shore. After hiding the canoes in the bushes, they ran behind Pierre into the woods.

"The Germans won't know what hit them when they see a lot of their food is gone." Lily laughed.

"Don't stop. We need to get deep into the forest," he shouted to the group. "And far away from houses and roads. We can stay at one of our huts. We'll be safe there for a while. The Germans haven't started to search the woods."

LILY

Soon Pierre raised his hand. "Okay, we're here. Let's rest for a while." He pulled back pine branches exposing the entrance to the makeshift dugout.

Lily and Rachel dropped to the ground and crawled into the deep and wide hole. They sat together leaning against its cold dirt walls. It was a large space. The ceiling was very low and covered with logs and branches from pine trees. No one was able to stand up in it, not even a child.

"This hut looks as if it could hold about eight people. They worked hard."

"We always do. We're are very patriotic and are trying to save our country from the Nazis," one of the boys said.

"We'll move again closer to midnight. Try to get some sleep. You'll be safe, don't worry. The group will take turns standing watch." Pierre pulled the branches over the entrance. "I'll take the first watch."

Lily whispered to her friend. "I guess we've joined the Partisans."

"Will we ever get back to our time?" Rachel murmured.

"I don't know. We have to take things as they come." Leaning on Rachel's shoulder and peering out of the entrance through the pine needles, she could see the pink and purple of the sky. *I'm in 1940 with my college roommate, a group of Partisans, and their leader, a French diplomat.* She laughed.

"Why are you laughing?" her friend asked.

"I'm laughing about our situation. Try to take a nap," she whispered to Rachel. "The sun is beginning to set. It will be dark before we know it."

Lily watched dusk slip into black sky. The moon was full and shone through the pine branches. She stared as Pierre rose from the front of the hut and found a tree. It made her feel safe as he leaned against it and watched the woods. Closing her eyes, she drifted into a fitful sleep.

Lily awoke when she heard the cracking of a branch. She crawled to the entrance and pushed away the pine branches to stare into the woods.

As her eyes met Pierre's, a shock ran through her. He was staring at her. For a moment she was speechless. *Does he suspect there is something strange about us?* These words jumped into her mind. "Is everything all right?" she asked.

"No. I was just wondering how you will work with us. Maybe I can get you to London for training."

"I think I would like that."

"Good. I'll make some arrangements."

"But right now I'm starved. Can't you hear my stomach growling?"

"Abraham, break out the bread and cheese," Pierre said to the young boy sitting next to him. He reached into the canvas bag the boy on sentry duty handed to him, took out a loaf of bread, and broke off a piece. Reaching into his pocket, he took out his knife and cut off a wedge of cheese. "What about Rachel?"

"I don't think anything will wake her."

"Don't the Partisans get sick of bread and cheese?"

"No, and most of them are Jewish. The food hasn't been blessed by the Rabbi, but they get so hungry they'll eat anything. I've even known them to eat pork sausage."

Lily hurriedly folded the cheese into the chunk of bread and took a bite. "Well, I can eat it. And it's so good. Bread and cheese were just what I needed." The food was finished quickly. "Boy, I could use a shower. The house is gone for us to use. Guess I'll have to wait a while for one."

"That's right, but we have several apartments in the village and the next town. We can go to one of them."

"What do you do with them?"

"We hide people in them. When we use the radios to send messages, we move them from place to place so the Germans have a hard time tracking us."

"Sounds dangerous." She stared at him. "What time is it?"

"Time to move to a safe place. Finish the food then wake up your friend. We have to go."

"Rachel." Lily crawled back into the hut and gently shook her.

"What? Where am I?" Rachel asked as she rubbed her eyes. "Oh that's right we're with the Partisans. Did I sleep long?"

"No. You took a short nap. Are you hungry?"

"No. I'm sick of bread and cheese. I'm going on a diet."

Lily looked around. Pierre had disappeared. "Remember, we're in 1940 and we've joined the resistance. We're moving from the woods and going to a safer place."

"Here, ladies...clothes from one of the boys." Pierre knelt on one knee, handing her a bag. "I'll wait outside while you change." Pierre threw the words over his shoulder as he left, covering the opening, and stood outside the hut.

"We're ready," Lily called. "Everything is a little big, but I rolled up the sleeves and pant legs to make them fit." She was beyond caring how she looked. It was comfort and warmth she was looking for. "Is there an empty canvas bag to put our clothes in?" She smiled and thanked him as he handed her one.

The bag was draped over her shoulder as she crawled out of the hut and stood up. "You never said exactly where we are going," Lily said moving to Pierre's side.

"Follow me. We're going into town to the convent. So far it's safe with the nuns. They will let us clean up and give us a bed for the night. At breakfast tomorrow we'll plan what our next move will be," Pierre said.

The group moved quietly through the woods. "When we leave the woods we have to cross an open space to get to the convent. So we'll have to be very careful." Pierre led them through the trees. Leaves and branches cracked under their feet. "Here we are. Wait here while I check and make sure it is clear." He moved from the woods and glanced around the convent grounds.

Lily waited with the group. She grabbed Rachel's hand. "Everything will be all right," he said returning to the woods. "We have to be very careful and move quickly. "All right everyone run," Pierre said as he led the group to the convent gates. "Stick together."

Within minutes the band of men and women gathered at the front gate of the convent. Pushing it open with just enough space for each one to squeeze through, they ran to the door of the nun's sleeping quarters.

Mother Superior threw open the door when Pierre knocked in code. "Hurry, the soldiers are patrolling tonight. They are making everyone open their doors. They force their way in and search." The nun ushered them into the chapel. "We have one room left in the tower. The men will have to hide and sleep in the barn. Don't forget to cover yourselves with hay." She opened the back door and peered around. "It's safe to go. Hurry." With open palms, she pushed the men out of the convent.

"Women and girls you can clean up in our quarters then go to one of the hidden rooms."

Lily's eyes followed Pierre as he left the convent. He turned to Lily and mouthed, *It will be okay.* She felt safe as she turned and trailed the nun back into the convent.

I need these. She took the towel and tooth brush the nun handed her.

Lily had just finished washing away the day's dirt and brushing her teeth and was beginning to feel more human when she heard pounding on the front door of the church.

"What is it?" the nun called out. "It's the soldiers," she whispered.

"Open up. We have a report people came to the convent tonight," a soldier yelled back.

"Just a minute…it's the middle of the night. Let me get dressed," the Mother Superior called out. "I'm coming. I will only be a minute."

"Quick," she whispered. "Come with me." The nun led Lily and Rachel and the women and teenagers to the chapel door that led from the sleeping quarters. Once in the chapel, she moved the tapestry behind the altar to the side and pulled on a hidden cord. A staircase lowered slowly into the chapel.

Lily heard the stairs scrape across the floor as it moved into the space next to the altar.

"Get up there." The holy sister pushed a button on the wall. A partition slid open. There were two sets of stairs. "The steps on my left go to the bell tower. These steps on my right go to small rooms. Go to the third room. There is still room. Don't talk. Tip-toe up the stairs. The soldiers won't be here very long. They're lazy. They just make a show of searching."

Lily was the last to enter the staircase. The wall slid closed behind her. Motioning for the group to go on, she turned and stopped, waiting on the first step as the soldiers pounded and hollered for the nun to come to the door.

She smiled when she heard the nun yell back at them with bridled anger in her voice. "All right. All right."

Her smile soon turned to a grimace. A chill ran through her when she understood the soldiers knocked at the pews and the confessionals with the butts of their guns.

"Who else is here?" a soldier yelled.

"No one is here except for the sisters. They should be asleep if you haven't awoken them," she shouted. "Now get out of here."

"All right. We are watching your convent. Your gate was open. Why is that?" one of the soldiers yelled. "Why is that?"

"One of the sisters must not have closed it when she came back from the Ghetto. I didn't check it tonight."

"See that you do. Anyone could sneak in and cause you harm. You should be very careful. We wouldn't want to drag you to one of the prisoner camps."

"Thank you for watching out for us."

Lily could tell the nun had her teeth clenched when she talked. She waited. When she heard the door slam and the quiet, she climbed the stairs to her assigned room. Reaching it, she looked around. The room was bare of furniture. Mattresses covered the wooden floor. No windows broke up the rough face of the walls, but she was able to see the moonlight through small thin slits at the top of the stone walls. Three young people and one elderly woman huddled against the back wall of the room, blankets thrown over their shoulders. They stared at Lily and the other new arrivals with frightened wide eyes. A dim light from a small lantern cast their shadows around the floor and the lower part of the room.

"It's all right. The soldiers are gone." Lily smiled. "Wait." Her index finger pressed to her lips. "Shush. I hear footsteps."

"Is everyone all right?" a woman's voice called out.

There were sighs of relief when the Mother Superior entered the room. She introduced Lily, Rachel, and the Partisans to the women standing at the back of the room as she handed out blankets and pillows.

"Have a woman and child arrived here yet? Their names are Gilda and Anna," Lily asked as Mother Superior finished.

"Not yet. I think they are due here tomorrow. The resistance leader told me to expect two more. To tell you the truth, your group is a surprise. We didn't expect you. But we have three rooms. These rooms will hold all of you and the three already here. A group of people has just left."

"We didn't expect to be here. I thank you very much for your help." Lily gave the nun a hug as she turned and started toward the doorway to leave the room.

"I didn't have time to tell you, but when I ring the bells, it means the German soldiers are approaching the convent. You have to be very quiet and get to the hiding place. When they are gone, I knock on the partition on this side of the bell tower." She smiled. "Get some sleep. Breakfast is at six a.m."

"How long have you been here? "Lily asked the women who stood beside a mattress.

"About two weeks," the woman answered. "These are my daughters." She pointed to the young women. "The men are in the barn. Partisans are making arrangements for us to be smuggled out of Poland and into Switzerland. We should be leaving soon."

"That will be quite a trip."

"The nuns take very good care of us. We were lucky to get out of the Ghetto, where we were being starved to death. The Germans have put restrictions on food coming into the Jewish quarters," she said as she laid down on her mattress and covered herself. The woman stuck her arm out. Reaching around Lily, she turned off the lantern. "Good night, ladies."

Lily dropped to the empty mattress in front of her. She turned and whispered to her friend. "It will be okay, Rachel. Tomorrow Pierre and the Partisans will help us find a safe place to stay.

The church was quiet. Daylight was approaching as the gray light of dawn shined through the cracks in the stones of the part of the bell tower she was in. A fog suddenly crept through the small slits and swirled around the room.

October 5, 2014

Lily pulled her covers up to her chin and stared around at her surroundings. A fog crept into the room too thick to see through. *I seem to be the only person in the room. This is too comfortable a bed to be a mattress on a wooden floor. This blanket is too soft to be the rough woolen one the nun gave me, and I didn't have a sheet.*

She closed her eyes tightly and opened them again. The fog had cleared. Looking around, she discovered she was back in the twenty-first century, warm and comfortable in the guest room of her friend's house. Rays of sun bounced off the glass mirror of the dresser across the room. Throwing back her covers and jumping out of bed, she tripped and stubbed her toe. As she bent down to rub it, she noticed a discoloration on her shin. "That's from when I tripped leaving the house. Pierre said I would have a bruise and I do. He was right." *I was in 1939 when it happened.*

Lily stood in her fancy underwear as she glanced at her clothes on the overstuffed chair as she walked to the side of the room. "My slacks are okay except for a little dirt on the right cuff. My shoes are a little scuffed up. It wasn't a dream. I did go back to the beginning of World War Two." She pulled a silk robe from a hanger in the armoire.

Lily wrapped herself in the robe and tipped-toed down the hall to Rachel's room. She stopped at the door and listened. It was quiet. As she continued on down the stairs and the hallway to the kitchen, she felt the cold tiles on her bare feet.

When she reached the doorway to the kitchen, she smiled. Anna was filling the French press with steaming water and pressing down on the floating coffee grounds. The last time she saw Anna was when she was a child with her grandmother in this kitchen during WWII. "Good morning," she called out to the housekeeper from the doorway.

Anna jumped.

"I'm sorry. I didn't mean to startle you. The coffee smells good."

"I was going to check and see if you were awake and bring you a cup."

"That's okay. I'll have it here." She pulled a chair away from the table. "I take it black."

"Miss Rachel isn't up yet. She usually sleeps late."

"Have you lived in Warsaw a long time?" Lily asked taking the cup from the housekeeper as she slid into the chair.

"Since I was a baby. I was born in Warsaw and lived in a beautiful home. My father was a doctor. I was about five years old when the Germans marched into Poland. Everything was all right for a while. But, soon the German soldiers started to round up all the Jews. They herded us to the Ghetto. We lived on grounds surrounded by a wall and wire fence. We were in a small apartment. I guess my parents knew what was happening and arranged for the nuns at the convent to smuggle me out and hide me. The nuns used to bring food to us. That's when they got me out. When the Germans made it harder and harder for us to get food even in the convent, they smuggled me out in an empty barrel in the wagon that brought in food."

"You were very lucky."

"You're right. They taught me the sign of the cross and lots of Catholic prayers and gave me false papers so if the Nazis questioned me they wouldn't know I was Jewish. When the convent and their orphanage filled up, Rachel's family hid me, then a family took me and pretended I was their child. Before I left the convent the nuns wrote out my family's names, put the paper in a glass jar with all the other names of children they'd rescued and buried it in the garden."

"That was a good idea. What happened to your parents?"

"They were taken to Auschwitz."

"What happened to you?"

"Toward the end of the war, the German soldiers invaded the house. I was dragged out of my room one day. I think someone reported the family. Probably a person who must have traded information for their freedom."

"Where did they take you?"

"They loaded me on the cattle car of a train with tons of other people. It was so crowded, we couldn't wait to leave it."

"What happened to the family that hid you?"

"They were shot right in front of me. I never knew what happened to their bodies. After I walked with a group of people to the cattle car, I was taken to a camp."

Lily winced as she shuddered, wrapping her arms around herself. *Anna never got out of Poland.*

"I wasn't at the camp a long time. Each time the guards in the camp gathered up people for the showers as they called them, women would hide me. I didn't understand, but I never objected because the women they took never came back to the barracks." She smiled.

"Anyway, after a couple of weeks, the American soldiers marched into the camp. They gave me some food from tins they carried in their packs. I think it was stew. It wasn't blessed by the Rabbi, but I didn't care I was so hungry. One of them gave me a chocolate candy bar. It was so good. I hadn't had chocolate since the beginning of the war. Food was very short when we were in the Ghetto and at the convent. The nuns and the family I was with served vegetables and potatoes and sausage and sometimes apples from the orchards around the town. Almost nothing was given to us to eat at the camp."

"What did you do after the war?" Lily asked as she watched Anna refill her cup.

"I had no place to go. I had one of the women who hid me in the barracks take me to the convent. The nuns remembered me but didn't know where my parents were.

They took me to the garden, dug up the jar, and gave me the slip of paper with my family name and where I had lived with my parents." She sighed. "Years later I searched for my parents. I could never find them. I finally gave up. I assumed they died at Auschwitz."

"How did you end up with Rachel's family?"

"I remembered they hid me during the beginning of the war. After a few weeks with the nuns at the convent, I found them. I've been with the family ever since."

"Good morning. I see Anna has given you coffee."

Lily turned toward the voice. "It's about time you got up." She watched Rachel pour herself a cup of coffee.

"At least I'm dressed."

"I should go and do the same."

"Wait, you can do that later. Grab your coffee. Let's go to the patio." Rachel motioned to Lily to follow her. "I need to talk with you."

Lily followed Rachel as she walked to the door off the back of the hallway. Chairs and a table on the patio mirrored the ones on her balcony.

When Rachel sat, she stared at the garden. "Were we really in 1939? I can't believe it."

"We were."

"Do you think we'll get another chance to go there again?"

"I hope so, Rachel. It was actually exciting."

"It's as if time stopped and we entered an alternative universe." Rachel smiled.

"Well, maybe it will happen soon. I'm not sure it will be tonight. Didn't you say Karl is coming? I don't think he's meant to go on our journey."

"Oh, I almost forgot to tell you. He won't be here tonight. He is going to be tied up in a meeting with the French Ambassador. He was very disappointed and will meet us at the Chopin concert. He called just before I ran to tell you to stay away."

"What happened?"

"The phone went dead. When I put the phone down, I glanced out the window. The sun was behind a cloud. A group of German soldiers was marching down the street on the road to our house. They stopped when a jeep carrying a German officer approached them. They were in front of the house. That's when I ran."

"How did you avoid them?"

"I left by the gardens, ran behind the shed, and through the woods. I didn't go very deep into the trees and could see you walking on the road. It was so real. That's when I called and ran toward you."

"It was strange, Rachel. We went back and were experiencing what happened after the German's invaded Poland and started World War II." Lily's eyebrows drew together. A chill ran up her spine.

"Miss Rachel." Anna appeared on the terrace with a plate of sweet rolls and the coffee press.

"Thank you, Anna. Just what I needed, a sweet roll?"

"More coffee?"

"Yes please," Lily said. Anna poured her another cup. "Thank you."

After Anna left, Lily smiled at Rachel. "Anna would never believe us if we told her we had seen her as a child. She must have been so traumatized she doesn't remember seeing us."

"No she wouldn't. Are you finished or do you want another roll?"

"No thanks. I bet I've gained weight already and I've only been here a few days."

Rachel began to gather up the cups and plates. "I don't need help." Anna waved Lily away from the table. "Go get dressed. I'll take you to the TV station. My show will be on. I taped it."

"Don't forget to gather up your clothes for tonight. We'll leave for Warsaw from the station."

"I need something to put my dress in."

"There's a clothing bag in the armoire."

"Where is your clothing?"

"I'll stop at the house in town and pick them up."

Lily looked around. Everything seemed so peaceful. Not like during the war. She didn't want to go back to 1940 just yet, even though she was curious about seeing more of what happened first hand. She was looking forward to the Chopin concert, cooking lessons, and what Rachel had planned for her visit.

CHAPTER FIVE

October 6, 2014

L ily stared out the window of the hallway at the river. *Are there people in the woods? Am I back in 1940 again?* "Rachel. Where are you?" she called walking through the kitchen and the opening of the side door.

"I'm outside waiting for you."

Lily watched Rachel press the button on her key ring, popping open the trunk of her car. She walked to the back of the car and laid her evening clothes in the clothing bag and her small bag carefully in the trunk. Before she walked to the passenger seat, she unzipped the case. The air was cool. Dragging a sweater from it, she closed the trunk lid. Throwing her sweater over her shoulders, she ran to her seat.

"It won't take us very long to get to the station."

"Do you think I'll get to meet Anika?"

"I hope so. She'll be doing the cooking part of her show live. I think she visited a local farm and taped it. That will be the first part of her show. The second part will feature a couple of soups with the fresh vegetables from the farmer's garden near the station."

Within minutes they were at the station.

Rachel pulled Lily to the stage where Anika's show was being filmed. "It's already started."

Lily sat, pulled out a pencil and pen, and took copious notes as Anika made her soups, red beet borscht and goulash.

When the program ended, Rachel grabbed Lily's hand and pulled her toward the chef "This is my friend, Anika. Lily, Chef Anika."

"I enjoyed your show and took notes. I work for a local newspaper in Paris. One of the reasons my editor was so happy to let me go on vacation was so I could write a column on Polish cuisine. I would love to interview you."

"That would be great. I'm trying to syndicate my program and get it on other stations in Europe. I'm seen pretty much throughout Poland."

"I also want to take a class from you at your school when you have time."

"Don't worry about that. Rachel and I are good friends. I could give you a private lesson or maybe one in the studio kitchen. Maybe I could put you on as one of my show's helpers."

"I told you she would do something special for us." Rachel smiled as she hugged her friend, the chef. "Anika you're great."

"Thanks. It will be fun. I'm looking forward to doing the show with you, Lily."

"Well, we have to get going. We're going to Warsaw and the Chopin concert and benefit tonight. When we get back we'll set up a time. Come on, Lily."

"I'll see you there," Anika called as Rachel and Lily rushed from the studio. "My company is catering the hors d'oeuvres for the Champagne Reception and after the concert, dessert, coffee, and liquors."

"You'll be busy supervising, but I hope you spare a few minutes to chat with us," Lily shouted over her shoulder.

"I'll try. See you later." Anika waved.

"It won't take long to get into Warsaw and our house. It's Wednesday. The traffic is not heavy in and out of the city on a weekday," Rachel said. "Did you bring your passport?"

"Yes. I always carry it with me now." The air turned cold, making her hug herself as she stared out into the countryside. Rachel, do you mind if I turn up the heat?"

"No. It's getting cool."

Lily felt a blast of warm air as she leaned over and turned the knob, changing the setting on the heater in front of her. The chill she was trying to get rid of wouldn't let go.

"We're at the house. It will only take me a minute. I got my things ready before I met you at the station. Everything is packed and in the front hallway. Our clothes won't get wrinkled if we change at the reception.

Lily waited while Rachel ran into the house. Within minutes she saw her friend at the trunk of her car. There was the familiar beep as the trunk lid opened. When it closed she watched Rachel run to her side of the car and jump in. Lily felt Rachel push her foot on the gas pedal and speed off to the reception and concert.

Lily stared at the large, bronze statue of Frederic Chopin as they entered Warsaw's Lazienki Park and Gardens. It was in the middle of the city of Warsaw. The history books tell the original statue was blown up by the Nazis. However, the Polish people were able to hide the original mold so the Germans couldn't destroy it. The mold survived the war and made it possible to cast a replica and place it back in the reflection pool.

LILY

Rachel drove slowly on the road to the country home of Polish royalty where the recital and reception party would be held.

Lily watched the peacocks roaming the grounds. Their bluish green feathers and the colorful almost five feet long tails of the males outdid the rather dull-colored female birds.

"Why don't they fly away?"

"They clip their wings." Rachel smiled.

"Be careful, Rachel, a peacock is on the road." Lily lurched forward as her friend's foot slammed down on her brakes.

"We're running late and that male bird has to take his time crossing the road." Rachel tapped on the horn of her car.

"You scared him." Lily watched him try to fly out of the way.

"Well, he's not traumatized and he moved a little faster didn't he?"

"He is reminded he can't fly. Who knows what kind of trauma he feels."

"Lily. Please give me a break. He's a bird."

"You were always impatient. Slow down. We're not late."

Rachel eased her foot off the brake and drove slower. When she reached the lake and crossed over the bridge, she drove to the lot on her left and pulled into a space near the back of the building. "Come on we need to get changed. Grab your clothes and follow me. I know an entrance at the rear of the building," Rachel said as she pushed on her key ring and opened the trunk of the car.

She led Lily to the ladies room behind the recital room.

"You look wonderful and very sophisticated in your black silk long pants and flowing top, Lily. It's stunning with your red hair. Are you ready?"

73

"Pale blue looks good with your blond hair," Lily said hanging her everyday clothes on the empty hanger. She glanced into the mirror. "Just a minute. I want to fix my makeup." She quickly refreshed her lipstick. Opening her compact, she dabbed powder on her nose. Pulling a comb out of her sequined evening bag, she ran it through her hair. "There, I'm done." Lily looked around and checked her bag to make sure everything was picked up and stuck back where it came from.

"We can leave the clothes we had on here. Karl will pick them up later." Rachel smiled.

Lily followed her friend through the music room and entered the front reception area. The guests in the area turned toward them.

"I think we're a hit," Lily leaned to her friend and whispered.

The staff dressed in black trousers, white, long-sleeved, stiffly starched shirts, and black bowties as they passed drinks and food. She smiled and took the fluted glass filled with champagne off the tray when the waiter approached her. "This must be French. Am I right, Rachel? I know the Pols are known for their vodka, not their champagne." Lily took a sip. "It is French and it is superb."

"You're right." Rachel laughed as she stared at the other side of the room. "There's Karl. He must have come right from work. I'll see if I can pry him away from his conversation. Be right back."

Lily watched her friend rush to her husband, kiss him on the cheek, and point to her. *They make a handsome couple.*

Karl looked across the room and waved. Just as he started toward her someone caught his arm.

Rachel waved and mouth, *we'll be right there.*

Lily stood looking at the painting hanging on the wall next to her as she sipped her drink.

"Hello."

"Hello." She turned toward the voice and the tray of hors d'oeuvres offered to her. "Anika. It's so good to see you again." Reaching into the middle of the tray, she took a cracker with an interesting topping. "What is this?"

"It's caviar with finely chopped hardboiled egg, onion, and a dab of sour cream."

"Are you working the party too?"

"I always help serve. That way, as I circulate, I can make sure my staff is doing a good job without being obvious."

"Now I know why you have such a good business."

"I know you and Rachel thought about taking my class, but I wondered if after I did my TV show I could come to her house and give a private lesson. I'll bring the food. I'm sure Rachel has all the pans and utensils I'll need. Do you want a dessert or main course?"

"I'll let Rachel know you'll be setting something up at her house and let her decide."

"Maybe we could do both. I'll pick dishes that are fairly easy and typical of Polish food. And we'll do the cooking at her house."

"Sounds good."

"I still think I should make you a guest on my show."

"Thanks. Then I can take a copy of the tape back to France and can check into getting your show on Paris television."

"That would be so kind of you." She smiled. "Well back to work."

Lily looked toward Rachel and Karl. Her friends were still tied up with the man who had approached Karl when he had started to her. Sipping on her drink, she strolled toward the opened door leading to the terrace and the gardens. With a glance at the sky, she passed couples sitting at the tables and chairs on the patio. The moon was full and bright. Torches had been placed on the lawn and path leading to the lake. The entire area was lit up showing the fall flowers. *The royal family had a wonderful life.*

Lily made a few notes on the Champagne Reception for the article she would send to her boss.

"There you are. We wondered where you disappeared to."

Lily turned, hearing her friend's voice. Rachel and Karl held hands as they walked toward her. She rushed to them. Giving Karl a hug, she smiled as he kissed both of her cheeks.

"Rachel has been doing nothing but talking about you and our college days since you emailed her you would be visiting," Karl said. "Our college days seem so long ago."

"Not so long ago," Lily said thinking for a moment. "Only fourteen years. But I saw you at your wedding thirteen years ago."

"That's right. Things were so hectic that day I forgot you were there. Rachel, I'm sorry. There's the French Ambassador. I need to ask him something."

"Karl, I'm going to introduce Lily to the pianist before the concert starts. We'll be right back." Rachel grabbed Lily's arm and pulled her to a woman dressed in a long, beige dress of satin embroidered material. The lace around the collar and end of the sleeves was the same color beige. *She appears to be in her eighties.*

"Madam Halina, this is my friend Lily. I'm so happy she is able to hear your concert. She timed her visit just right."

"Where are you living?"

"I'm living in Paris, France."

The woman smiled. "I learned to play the piano when I was a very small child in France. My family and I escaped to the French countryside in 1942. We lived there, or I should say hid there after the Germans occupied the country until the war ended. I came back to my country when it was over and have been here ever since. I loved France but there's nothing like home."

Lily saw the lights dim.

"Well, it's time for the concert to start. It was nice to meet you, Lily. I hope you enjoy your visit." The woman rushed into the room and sat at the piano.

"Shall we get a seat?" Lily asked Rachel as she stood in the doorway with her friend. Looking around, she quickly set her glass on a small tray on the table next to her and started into the recital room.

"I spoke to Anika and she is going to give us a private lesson at your home," Lily whispered to Rachel as Karl joined them. "Where are our seats?" Lily asked.

"I'm the committee chairperson so we get to sit in the front row."

"I didn't know I was in the company of such an important person." Lily sat next to her friend and preceded to get lost in the music.

When the concert was over, Lily rushed to Madame Halina as she walked to the entrance where the coffee and sweets were being served.

"The concert was wonderful. I enjoyed it, Madam Halina. It reminded me of my grandparents. We always heard Chopin's music playing in their home."

"Thank you very much. It's nice to meet you. I'm afraid I have to leave. My driver is waiting. I can see him at the bottom of the stairs." Madame Halina pointed out the open front door to the man standing beside a long limo.

Lily waved as the woman left.

"She was in a hurry," Lily said as Karl and Rachel joined her.

"I think being elderly makes it hard for her to stand and chat for a long time. So, she usually leaves right after the concert."

Lily smiled as Anika arrived at their side and asked, "A sweet?"

"Thank you. I'll just have coffee," she said as she walked to the table with coffee cups and saucers. "Oh, I forgot. I'm going to write an article on what you served at the event."

"Well, Karl was looking forward to visiting with you," Rachel announced.

"Aren't you coming back to the house with us?"

"I have to stay in town. There are some problems in my office, but we'll spend a few days together before you leave."

"Marvelous," she said giving him a hug.

"Wait, you have to taste one of the desserts and tell me what you think before you go so I can use it for my article."

"I'm going to take one with chocolate and one with lemon," he said as he described them after he ate. Rachel described what she thought about her selections.

"All right. Lily pulled a pad from her purse. "Let me write the descriptions of the hors d'oeuvres and sweets you both had."

Rachel gave Karl a kiss. "See you soon."

"Are you finished? Come on, Lily, forget the coffee. Put your pad away. Let's take a little walk before we start back to the house."

"Wait. Just one more word."

October 30, 1941

"It's starting to get foggy," Lily said as they walked across the street and passed the museum of Jewish antiquity. "We better get to your car. The fog is getting so heavy I can barely see my hand holding it in front of my face."

"It's too bad it's so late and the museum is closed. You would enjoy it. It was built on the property where the

Ghetto was. The Ghetto was destroyed before the end of the war by the Nazis and stayed empty until there was enough money to honor the people who lived and died there."

"The fog is beginning to clear. We can at least see the outside of the buildings," Lily said. "Oh no. We're back in World War II. I see ghostly shapes moving through the mist." Lily stared ahead at the haggard, thin men and women in loosely fitted tattered clothes with yellow stars sewn to their chests. A man, with sunken eyes, looked at her gravely and pointed behind her. When she turned, she saw decaying gravestones and the piles of stones that had been a synagogue.

"I see a brick wall with barbed wire running along the top of the wall," she said breathing deeply as she looked away. "Come on, let's go look through the gate."

"No. It's dangerous." Rachel didn't move.

"It's just a wood frame with wire covering it." Lily stumbled as she pulled Rachel behind her to the gate.

"We've got to get out of these evening clothes. My heel caught in the hem of my silk slacks."

"Where can we go? My car won't be where I left it. Remember we're not in 2014 anymore. We have to be careful. Soldiers are patrolling the perimeter with dogs." She got close to the front of the gate and stared. "Look at the people laying on the ground. They look as if they are starving."

"I can see some nuns carrying baskets and handing out food. Maybe they can help us." Lily pointed to the nun near her and motioned for her to walk with her on the way out of the Ghetto. "She's wearing a very large habit, her cornette is long and hangs down her back. The basket looks heavy, but she looks strong and her sturdy, black, squared heeled shoes seem to allow her to walk without trouble. It doesn't look as if she would fall no matter how heavy her hamper is."

"The Germans let the nuns go in the Ghetto, for now, to help the sick and deliver food. They have special permits. I'm not sure how long the soldier will let this go on," Rachel said. "The nuns give away the food for free because the people in the Ghetto are only allowed to have fifty dollars of their money a week."

"It looks as if some people get more rations than others."

"That's right. The ones who work as laborers for the Nazis get a thousand calories a day the others get three hundred calories."

"That's terrible."

"It's bad for everyone behind the walls. They live in two and a half room apartments with six people per room. The conditions are dreadful. The people suffer from disease and starvation."

"Here comes one of the nuns. Oh, it's Mother Superior." Lily stepped back as she watched the sister push open the gate. "Your basket looks heavy. May I help you? You seem to be having difficulty carrying it."

"No thank you. My wagon is right behind you across the street. I'll be there in a minute."

"Wait here, Rachel." Lily caught up to the nun just as she lifted the basket, pushing it into the back of the wagon. *Is that a child's voice?* "Sister, who is that?"

The nun put her index finger to her lips. "Shush, shush. I'll tell you, but you must never tell anyone or talk about it."

"I promise I won't." She leaned close to the nun.

"I have a small child curled up in the basket. We smuggle them out of the Ghetto one at a time and hide them in the church until we can find families for them or get them out of Poland. The sisters teach them the catechism and how to cross themselves so the soldiers don't know they are Jews or one of the few Gypsies that are also forced into the Ghetto," the nun whispered.

"Are you able to help a lot of people?"

"A lot, but not as many as we would like." The nun lifted the blanket and patted the child.

"We have people who make false papers before we take them to a country that is not occupied by the Nazis. The people you saw in the bell tower were smuggled out by Pierre and his group. One of the nuns goes with the group if there are children."

"Where do they take them?"

"We usually go to Sweden by boat or over the mountains to Spain or Switzerland. I can't talk anymore. I have to go before the soldiers on patrol get here and check on me."

"All right. I'm sure you'll be seeing me again." Lily stood back as the nun jumped into her wagon and whipped her horses. She watched her drive in the direction of the convent. When the wagon disappeared, she ran to Rachel.

"What was she saying to you?"

Just as Lily began to answer, she heard a noise. Glancing sideward, she saw a man in a calf-length, black trench coat and a dark fedora step from the shadows. She nudged her friend.

"Don't get upset, Rachel. Stay calm. We have company. A Gestapo man, who must have been lurking in the shadows, is now walking toward us."

"Ladies, there is a curfew. Why are you out on the street?"

"We were at a restaurant near here. Our car broke down just as we started to leave for home. Since we live close by, we decided to walk. We thought we would have time to get home before the curfew started." Lily hoped he would believe her and wouldn't check up on her explanation.

"What were you doing with the nun?" he barked at the girls.

"We were just helping her. Can't you see she's elderly?"

"Crazy woman. Helping those awful people. Papers!" He stuck out his hand.

Lily opened her purse and pulled out her passport. As she handed it to him, she glanced at her friend who shuffled through her purse, her hand shaking. Lily held her breath, wondering if she should offer to help. She heaved a sigh of relief when Rachel pulled her passport out of her bag and handed it toward him.

He examined her information before he grabbed Rachel's document.

"You're from France. On a visit?"

Lily nodded.

"We'll be there soon." He handed Lily her passport.

His contemptuous tone infuriated her. It was the same thing the soldier on the train had said. A warning voice whispered in her head. *Don't say a word.* She swallowed hard.

He took Rachel's passport from her hand. "Are you from France also?" he turned and asked Rachel.

"No, from here." Rachel inhaled and held her breath, hoping he wouldn't recognize her name as being Jewish. When he scanned her passport, she exhaled, realizing he barely glanced at it. She stuffed it into the pocket of her coat when it was returned.

"I'll let you go this time. Next time if it's past curfew I'll have to take you to Gestapo Head Quarters and interrogate you," he called over his shoulder as he walked away.

"What's that supposed to mean? Why can't he accept we're just a little late after having a nice evening? We weren't doing anything nefarious."

"Lily, calm down." Rachel seized her friend's arm. "We are on our way and he's disappeared. We have to be careful." Rachel grabbed her arm tighter and dragged her away from the Ghetto. "Walk quickly. You've looked enough."

Lily glanced over her shoulder at the people in front of the closed gate. Their ragged clothes hung on them. Their cheeks were sunken, their arms and legs were covered with only skin, no fat or muscle. There was a look of defeat and despair in their eyes.

"Ladies," a voice whispered as they turned the corner.

Lily stopped as a tall figure stood in front of a doorway and blocked their way as they left the Ghetto.

"Lily. What's going on?" Rachel asked as she stumbled into her friend.

"It's Pierre." Lily gripped her friend around the waist before she fell.

"What are you doing out after curfew? You should know better," he said.

"We had dinner in a restaurant in the park and lost track of time. We were on our way to Rachel's apartment in the city square. It's just around the corner."

"I'll walk with you. We'll take the back alley to the street. It will only take a few minutes."

"Oh no!" Rachel cried when they arrive at the building where her apartment was located.

"What's wrong?" Lily asked.

"Soldiers are guarding the building. There's a Nazi flag hanging from a pole over the door of our apartment. What are we going to do? Who can help us?"

"Stay calm, Rachel."

"Everyone in the apartment has been safe up to now, but the Nazi's have taken it over. Who knows what happened. They are getting stricter and taking more and more property," Pierre said.

"What do you think happened to the people who lived in our apartment and the other apartments in the building? Do you think they took them to the Ghetto?" Rachel sighed.

"Hopefully they escaped to the countryside when they realized what was going on and the Nazis were coming."

"I'll get you a place to stay. We have a safe house just outside of town. You can stay there tonight."

"Thank you," Lily said. "We'll need to borrow some clothes again. I hope you don't mind."

"Of course not. We'll go to the convent tomorrow and see if the nuns can find out where your relatives are. I hope not in the Ghetto."

"We keep meeting so let me ask, do you ladies still want to join the Partisans? If you do, you're going to need some training. We have a plane from London landing here tomorrow night. We'll be going to the SOE, Special Operations Executives, at 54 Baker Street in London. That's where everyone is trained."

"Will you be going?" Lily asked.

"I sure will. I help with the training. It usually takes eight months, but they have crammed everything into two months because the war is expanding through Europe."

"That's not very long."

"It's very intense." He stopped at a large, bombed out, gated building. "Here we are. I have to go back to the woods. There's a guard at the gate. You can't see him, but push the button on the wall and he'll appear." He pointed to the wall in front of him. "Tell him I sent you, and that you need some clothes, plus a place to sleep. You can pick up some more suitable stuff when we get to England. High heels and fancy dresses aren't exactly the things for resistance workers."

CHAPTER SIX

October 1, 1942

L ily sat at the convent dining table in front of a large fireplace with the nuns. She set her coffee cup in its saucer and stared at the tapestries on the walls. The Germans hadn't looted the convent yet. Soon the nun's silver, tapestries, and other precious articles would be gone. Suddenly she felt cold and picked up her coffee in both hands. Her fingers warmed as she drained the cup, but she still felt a chill move up her back as she thought about what was to come. With her eyes lowered, she stared into the fire. *Should I tell them? No, let them live without worrying about what's to come.*

"Oh. What is it, Mother Superior?" startled by footstep, Lily looked up and asked.

"I brought you some long pants, boots, a shirt, and a jacket. You can go change in the room next to this one."

"Thank you for the clothes." The nun placed the neatly folded pile into her arms. "Please keep our dresses."

"Yes, dear. Now go change. Hurry. You'll be joined by some other Partisans and will be leaving."

"I thought we were going to a safe house."

"Not tonight. It's clear and will be safe for a plane to land and fly you to London."

Lily stuffed the makeup from her purse into the pockets of clothes the nun brought her after she changed. "Please put this with my dress." Pulling a pad of paper out of her purse, she handed the sister her purse. "Where's Rachel?"

"Already changed and waiting for us."

"Come on, we're going to smuggle you in a wagon filled with hay, you'll be taken to the makeshift airfield in the western end of the city."

Lily wondered if they would get to the plane without being caught by soldiers patrolling the area.

"All right. Follow me." Mother Superior led her to the barn.

"It's going to be all right," Mother whispered to Lily.

"I really hope so." Lily smiled. She helped pull Rachel up on the wagon next to her. Laying down, she pushed into the hay and looked around. Only three of Pierre's group was with them. *I guess the others have been trained.* With the hay pulled over her, as the others did, she whispered, "Am I covered, Mother Superior?"

"You're fine. No one can see you."

When the wagon stopped, Lily stuck her head out of the hay, scanned the scenery, and seeing only people she knew, she jumped out. Brushing hay from her hair as the group moved briskly through the tangle of high grass and weeds and uneven ground. The group stopped and she sat in the cover of trees. Closing her eyes, she fell into a light sleep waiting for the plane to arrive. Jarred awake by the roar of a plane flying overhead, she listened as the plane's engines slowed. Within a few minutes, she heard its wheels bounce on the rough ground. The moon was full now. The clouds had cleared. She stared at Pierre when he arrived and spoke to the young man who had lent them some clothes when she first met the group. It was hard for her to see his face. Did he seem worried? Stopping her staring abruptly, she began to shake.

"What's wrong? You look terrified." Pierre walked toward her.

"I think I hear motorcycles."

He listened for a moment. "You're right, but they're on the main road and will be gone before we take off. We're in the middle of a clearing in the middle of the forest and the noise of their motorcycles won't allow them to hear the plane's engine as it idles. They haven't found this place yet, but we still have to hurry. The plane has to take off quickly." Giving her his hand, he drew her to her feet and pulled her into his arms, patting her on the back. "It's all right. They're still far enough away for us to have time to reach the plane and for it to take off. Run." He stared at Lily.

"Where are the rest of your group, and where's Rachel?"

"She decided to go back to the convent and help with the groups of people the nuns try to save and take to neutral countries. Don't worry she'll be all right. Her message to you is that she will see you when we get back. As for the men, they're on the plane."

Lily knew she would see Rachel when she got back to the year 2014, but she still shook. Fear knotted inside her. Even taking a deep breath didn't help her feeling of nervousness recede. *I won't believe I'll be safe until the plane takes off and we're on our way to England.* Grateful for his strength when his arms encircled her, she began to move quickly with him toward their ride to London.

One of the men already standing in the plane pull her up. The others slid to the end of the bench being used as a seat, so she could sit down. Hearing the sound of the propellers spinning and feeling no movement of the plane, she became nervous. "What's going on?"

Pierre backed down the stairs and looked under the plane. "It's stuck in the mud," he yelled to the pilot. "Send the men out and we'll try to push it out of the deep rut holding it to the ground."

Lily glanced at her watch wondering if she would be captured, never getting to help with the resistance or getting back to her real life. An icy fear twisted around her heart. Her stomach clenched tight. Anxiety spurted through her. Leaning back against the wall of the plane, she took a deep breath. *Relax.* She tried to believe the plane would move in time and forced her nerves to stop jumping in her chest. As she watched out the window, she saw the plane wheels spinning and the mud flying. Drawing a deep breath, she forbade herself to tremble and waited with tightly closed eyes. Her hands clenched into fists as she felt the plane rocking. It didn't move forward. Finally, she heard the pilot shut off the motor. *What's happening? No one has told me to leave the plane.* She was afraid to ask.

When she glanced out the window, she saw a man run across the field toward the forest. Soon she heard the sound of voices. A quick glance at her watch reminded her an hour had passed since she'd left the convent. It was still dark and the sky was clear. As she turned and stared out of the window to see what was happening. A group of men running beside a wagon, being pulled by oxen, neared the plane. A cry of relief escaped her lips as she watched them attach the wagon to the front wheels of the plane and urge the oxen to move forward. In a few minutes, the plane began to move.

Pierre jumped on the plane and sat beside her. "We'll be underway in a few minutes."

She exhaled. Only an hour and several minutes had passed. It seemed as if it had been hours. She stared out the window as the group of men ran off into the woods and the driver of the wagon steered the oxen to a path leading to the other side of the field. The plane taxied down the field and lifted off within minutes. The power of relief filled the air.

Her apprehension subsided when she saw Pierre drop down in the seat next to her as the plane lifted off the ground and roared into the night.

"Don't worry, we'll get to our destination safely. We left just in time. It's going to be light pretty soon. The Germans are busy and won't start to patrol close to the area for another hour. In the dark, they won't see a plane."

October 2, 1942

"It's time to wake up."

"We're here already? I didn't even feel us land. I guess I fell asleep." Lily sat up alone except for the pilot standing over her. A glance out the plane window surprised her as she shook off her grogginess. The plane had landed at an airfield filled with military planes, and uniformed people, trucks, and jeeps on the ground around the plane. Pierre was nowhere in sight.

"Where are Pierre and the others?" A soft gasp escaped her.

"The others are with him. He had to make contact with his boss. He arranged for the driver to take you to your hotel. The car is just outside the hangar at the end of the airfield to your left. It's just a short walk." The pilot glanced at his watch. "It's eight a.m. He said he would pick you up at noon tomorrow." He smiled.

"Thank you. Maybe I'll see you on the way back."

"Probably," the pilot said. "The trip back and forth to Poland seems to be my job."

Lily smiled. She stared at her surroundings as she climbed down the steps of the plane. Turning, she walked toward the soldier standing beside a sedan marked with letters spelling out British Army. *My mouth is so dry. I need to brush my teeth.* It was a cool morning. Lily wrapped her arms around herself.

"I'll turn on the heat in the car as soon as we get started, Miss. It will warm up quickly."

"Thank you. How long is the trip to the hotel?" Lily asked when she stood in front of the boxy four-door car.

"About an hour. We're outside of London."

Lily watched as the driver pushed on the handle and pulled open the door. He handed her an envelope. "Your friend left you some pounds in case you need anything."

He slammed the door of the car after she climbed into the backseat and settled in. Peeking into the envelope, she realized he knew she would want to change out of her clothes and put a new outfit together. *There will be time to buy a few things before dinner tonight.* Lily smiled again fingering through the bills. *He's very generous.*

When they arrived at the London city limits, she stared out the window at the city as they drove. It was rush hour. Cars were maneuvering in and out of traffic as drivers honked their horns once in a while. Everyone on the sidewalks seemed to be in a hurry as they traveled in one direction or the other. Two-decker red buses stopped at the corners and picked up passengers.

Amazed, she took a good look at the way the people dressed. They were clothed in somber colors. The men wore suits with sweater vests over shirts and ties. Their trousers had no cuffs and fedora hats protected their heads. The women also wore clothes in somber dark colors. Many had on two-piece suits. The jackets had padded shoulders and were boxy. The skirts were straight and reached below the knees. Others had on shirtwaist dresses with narrow belts around their waists. They wore stockings with a black seam up the back or ankle socks. If they wore a jacket over their dress, it looked like the suit jackets. Many wore hats. The shoes were clumpy platform *Frivolous and glamorous styles seem to be out. Don't think I'll be buying much.*

When the car stopped, she looked out at a small white cement hotel with a revolving side door. There were small balconies in front of glass pane French doors on each floor. The next door building had been bombed. Rubble was piled in a deep hole. Black soot covered the sidewall of the hotel where she would stay. *The hotel was lucky. It was spared damage except for some dirt.*

The driver opened his door, jumped out, and ran to her side of the car. He opened the door, helped her out, and walked with her through the revolving door to the desk. The soldier whispered to the clerk as he stood beside her.

"Miss O'Malley, we've been expecting you. We have your reservation for one night." The clerk reached behind him pulling out a brass key from a slot. "Room thirty-two. Mr. Girard said he would be back for you tomorrow morning." *He didn't ask about luggage. He must be used to my type of client.*

I guess I'll be starting my training right away. But first I need some clothes.

"Do you happen to have a toothbrush and paste I could purchase?" she asked as she looked at the clerk behind the desk.

"We provide a bath kit. You'll find it in the bathroom of your room."

"Thank you."

Lily looked at the elevator and decided to walk up the one flight of stairs to her room. She walked across the gray marble tiled floor to the circular staircase. Holding onto the brass rail as she climbed, she looked back over her shoulder when she reached the landing. *The lobby is quiet. I'm sure it busies up at noon.*

"Thirty-one, thirty-two. Here we are." She slipped the key into the lock of door thirty-two and turned it. Peering in, she smiled. The bedspread and pillows were royal blue and ivory. The drapes were satin in the same royal blue. The armoire, table, and chair were mahogany. An overstuffed chair in royal blue sat next to the window. The bench at the end of the bed was covered in the same color as the drapes. An ivory carpet covered the floor of the room. She walked to the closed door next to the armoire. Opening it, she saw the bathroom.

"Thank goodness, a toothbrush." She ripped the kit open, squeezed paste on the brush, and brushed her teeth. "Oh, that feels so much better. Shower time after shopping."

The door clicked and locked automatically as she let the handle slip from her hand. She ran down the stairs to the desk clerk. "Did I pass a women's clothing shop a little ways down the block from the hotel?"

"Yes, Miss. It's at the end of the block across from the underground train entrance. Turn left when you leave the hotel. There's another shop two stops on the tube from the shop you asked about. There's another shop, but you have to get on the underground train. Go two stops east. It will be on your left when you get to the top of the tube exit.

"Thanks." Sliding the key toward him she walked quickly, pushing through the revolving door. *The sidewalk has cleared a bit. I guess most of the people have reached their destination and are hard at work. Soon I'll be in training and also hard at work.*

The stores were beginning to open. She stood near the entrance of the one she wanted to enter, waiting for someone to come along and open up. "I'll come back to the station, ride the two stops and try the other store after I see what I can find here," she said as she looked across the street at the underground station.

"I'll be open in a minute," a woman said.

Lily smiled as she watched her turn the key in the lock of the shop's door. After Lily heard the click of the key and observed her push the door open, she waited a few seconds and followed her in.

"Good morning, Miss," the woman said as she pulled off her coat, hanging it on a hook near the front door and walked behind the glass counter. "I'll be right with you." The woman smiled.

"Good morning." Lily smiled, glancing down at the counter. *Don't get distracted, Lily. You need clothes. Costume jewelry comes last.* "Take your time. I'm interested in slacks, blouses, and sweaters. I'm not in a hurry. I'll just look around while you get settled." She was glad the clerk didn't mention her clothes or ask her any questions about how she was dressed. It would be hard to know what to answer.

After several minutes, the woman came around the counter and stood next to Lily. "All right. Now, what can I help you with?"

"I see everything is made with artificial fibers."

"Yes. Since the war began nothing is made of wool or linen anymore. We don't even have much cotton."

"Well, let's see, this suit seems nice." Lily took it from the rack and held it up to herself. "I think this might fit," she said walking to the floor to ceiling mirror and looking at herself.

"It looks like your size, but why don't you try it on. The dressing room is in the back. Follow me."

"Maybe I'll try it on with a blouse. Let's see. Perhaps a white and pale blue will go with navy." After she changed, she looked at herself in the mirror. *It fits perfectly. I really don't like the padded shoulders or the boxy shape of the jacket, but it's the style.* She shrugged her shoulders. Sticking her head out of the door to the dressing room, she called to the woman. "Could you bring me that pair of black slacks and a tan jacket next to the rack with the slacks, please?"

In a few minutes, she walked out of the fitting room with the clothes she wanted hanging over her arm. She laid them on the counter and peered at the price tags then into the envelope holding the pounds Pierre left for her. *He left me enough.*

"Anything else?" the clerk asked. "Maybe a fur coat. It's cool some days."

"What kind of fur is it?"

"It's Coney rabbit that is dyed to look like mink."

"I think I'll pass on the coat, but maybe some underwear and a pale blue, long sleeve sweater. I think the sweater will keep me warm if I wear it under the jacket. I can tell it's wool," she said.

"Yes. That's one of the wool sweaters done before we got involved in the war."

Lily watched the woman pull out some fancy underwear from the cubby holes behind her and thumb through it.

"I don't have any underwear in your size. I'm all sold out and don't know when I'll get a shipment in. The war has slowed everything down."

"We knit gloves for the soldiers. Wool is the only thing we use. Everything else is nylon or some kind of synthetic material."

Lily looked around. "Thanks. Think I have everything I need for now," she said watching the clerk fold her clothes and slide them into a brown paper bag. She laid the envelope on the counter and pulled out some money, Lily added up the cost from the sales tags and handed the clerk the pounds. "I think that will do." She picked up the envelope, folded it, and stuffed it in her pocket.

"Just right. Sorry, I don't have a fancier bag, but with the war, everyone is trying to cut costs."

"It's fine. Thank you. Have a good day." Hearing the jingle of a bell over the door as it opened, she waved, holding onto the door handle as it slowly closed. When she headed to the underground train a double decker red bus passed by. She smiled and waved to the people on the upper deck. *Next time I visit London, I'm going for a ride on one of those.*

Looking at the white sign with black block letters at the entrance, she read, *Designated Air-Raid Shelter.* At the top of the down escalator, she stepped on the moving stairs. As it moved her to the platform and the rails beneath the street, she understood. *That's why the English used these areas as shelters when the Germans bombed London.* The tracks of the underground were at least two hundred feet deep.

When she reached the platform, she stood and watched a man handing out tickets. When she heard him yell at her, she turned in his direction.

"Hey, lady, want a ticket? You'll be safe if you come down here at night in case a bomb falls. Only people with tickets can come down here. We even serve tea and food."

"How much?"

"No cost. It's war time."

"I'll think about it. Right now, I have someplace to go." She smiled waving as she jumped on the train when it stopped. The train was filled with passengers, but she found a seat next to an elderly woman who was humming to herself.

Staring at the walls through the glass windows of the tube as they thundered through the tunnel, she read the graffiti. It all said things about the Nazis and the soldiers bravely fighting them. Lily thought about what she was about to do with the Partisans. *Hopefully, my hotel won't get bombed. Maybe I should have taken a ticket. No, I'll be all right.*

Her stop came quickly. "Do you need help?" Lily asked joining the woman, who struggled with a large bag, as she walked to the door and left the train.

"I'm just going up to the street. I live near the station."

Lily grabbed the bag, holding it and hers in the same hand. She took the woman's arm and helped her step onto the escalator, holding on to her arm while the stairs moved upward.

"Are you helping the soldiers? I noticed you're dressed like them."

"Something like that."

"You're not English."

"No, I'm from the United States." Not feeling like going into where she lived now, she let that be her answer.

"We're in the middle of a war. You should go home on the next boat."

"I'm thinking about that." Lily smiled.

When they reached the street, Lily helped the woman step off the escalator.

"Thank you, dearie. Have a good day," the woman said as she grabbed her bag and turned to her left.

Lily smiled and waved goodbye to her. She watched until the woman crossed the street and waited until the woman disappeared into a building next to the store where she was going. *She's all right.*

The tinkling of a bell as she opened the boutique's door made her smile. "Good morning." She stared at the man behind the counter.

"Good morning. What can I help you with?"

"I need a pair of shoes, stockings, and maybe a pair of black ankle socks and some fancy under things." Lily glanced at the glass shelves on the wall. "And a bright colored scarf, please." *That will brighten up my outfits. The one on the first shelf with shades of blue and green will be perfect.* After she selected a pair of, black, clumpy wedge, heeled shoes, stockings, and socks, and underwear she paid. "I don't need a bag you can put them in this one." She held up the bag with her other purchases. "Thank you."

"Things are very reasonable," she said to herself as she walked to the tube station. "I forgot it's 1940. I will be so glad to get in the shower, wash my hair, and get into my new clothes," she whispered sitting on an almost empty train on her ride to the hotel. When she reached her stop, she looked around, the man had left. *I guess he gave all the tickets away.*

Glancing at her watch, she smiled. "I still have an hour before dinner. She tossed the bag with her clothes on the bed and dropped the clothes she wore on the floor and headed for the shower. *I'm glad to get rid of the things I was wearing.* Waiting for the water to warm up, she climbed over the side of the tub and stood under the shower until the water cooled. Grabbing the large, towel next to the tub, she dried herself, dressed in her new underwear, slacks, white blouse, and tan jacket. After she put her scarf under the collar of her jacket letting the ends hang in front, she applied her makeup.

She looked down at the floor. *Oh no, I almost forgot. Where is my head?* She slipped on her ankle socks and new shoes. Staring into the mirror on the back of the room door as she left, she smiled. *I feel human again and no one would know I'm not a person living in the 1940s.* After it slammed shut, she pulled down on the door handle checking to make sure her room was locked before she made her way to the lobby. *Why did I do that? I know it locks automatically.* When she reached the lobby, she sat near the front desk and read a magazine while she waited for the small restaurant in the hotel to open.

As soon as she saw a man in a black suit stand near the open doors of the restaurant, she rushed to the doorway and was the first to be seated. A quick look at the few choices on the menu the man handed her made her realize there were shortages everywhere. When the waiter approached her table, she ordered. "Fish and chips look good. Also a glass of white wine. Please." Realizing this was the first meal she'd had all day, her dinner quickly disappeared.

After dinner, she decided to take a walk and look around the immediate area of the hotel. The streets were empty. Soon, she felt herself yawning and decided to return to the hotel. Before she walked very far, she heard the siren of the air-raid warning as she reached the steps.

"That means bombs are going to fall." She watched everyone on the street run. "Oh. I should have gotten one of the tickets in the underground station. Too late now. Rushing back through the revolving doors, she heard the desk clerk yelling at the people in the lobby.

"Get to the basement," the clerk yelled. When he saw her turn toward the elevator, he yelled again. "Take the stairs." He pointed to the door saying exit.

She threw it open and ran down until she reached a large room in the basement. People had already started to congregate. They all sat listening to the bombs hit buildings. One girl started to cry. Lily moved close to her. "It will be all right." Reaching for the girl's hand, she held it. Finally, the sirens went silent and the all clear signal went off. The air-raid was over. Lily climbed the stairs to the first floor. Pushing on the door, she looked around the lobby, then walked through the revolving door to the front steps. *Oh my gosh. Bombs hit the buildings across the street.*

"The bombing is probably over for tonight." The desk clerk smiled at Lily.

"It's my bed time," she whispered as she made her way back to her room. Before going to bed, she placed the clothes she had on when she arrived in a laundry bag and left them outside her door so they would be picked up and cleaned while she slept. Glancing at the bed, she went over to it and crawled under the duvet falling asleep as soon as she shut her eyes.

When she woke, she showered, wrapped her towel around her, and then packed the clothes she had worn the evening before in the bag with the other new ones. Opening her room door, she found the clothes she had arrived in cleaned and pressed, so she dressed in them.

She ran down the stairs and stood at the desk with her key in her hand when she saw Pierre stroll through the revolving door.

"Wow, you look nice and rested."

"Thanks for the money. I'll pay you back. I wore my new clothes last night for dinner."

"Don't worry about it. It's on the Brits. I knew you would want to get out of those clothes you were wearing for a while. But, never fear. It will be only your old ones as you go through training."

"I didn't buy a lot. I passed on the hat and gloves and the rabbit fur coat. Just two outfits." She dropped her key on the desk.

"Come on." Pierre grabbed her hand. "We need to get to the SOE and MI6."

After she followed him through the twirling doors, he led her down the stairs and hailed a black cab when they reached the curb. "Fifty-four Broadway," he said to the driver as they got into the cab. When they settled, he turned to Lily. "We're going to MI6 then to SOE."

Driving through London, she listened to his description of the people she would meet and the different functions of the two organization.

"So...MI6, or Military Intelligence section six, codes and decodes messages, does radio work, and obtains intelligence. The SOE attacks, assassinates, blows up the enemy or their trains, factory, buildings, power plants, bridges, cuts phone lines, and so on."

"You've got it." The cab stopped in front of a cement building that appeared as an ordinary office building. "Follow me. Room fourteen is at the back of the building. I need to pick up some papers." He turned to the driver. "Wait."

Lily smiled as she was introduced to the MI6 men sitting behind desks and who would be training her at SOE. Her instruction would be very intense but not the end of all the things she needed to know. She would be learning the basics. A lot of her training would be on the job. Two months of training would go fast.

Her room would be at the mansion on the grounds of the camp at Benchley Park, outside London.

"I'll pick you up at the end of the training," Pierre said walking toward the cab. "By the way, you'll find more uniforms in your room at the mansion." He threw the words over his shoulder as he neared the cab.

Lily watched him bend down and whisper something to the cabbie.

"The driver knows where to take you."

"Aren't you going to stay and supervise me?"

"No. I have some work to do in London, but I'll be flying back to Poland with you."

Lily jumped into the rear seat. As the car moved, she turned and stared out the back window of the taxi and waved as Pierre disappeared into the crowded street.

Her talent of reading people made that part of the education easy. For part of her training, she learned the German ranks and their uniforms and parts of the trains. The hardest part of training was the thirty-mile hike and mountain climbing. This was done to help her get into shape. Bomb making was touched on but was part of the on-the-job training. She enjoyed learning to use a radio to send and receive messages. The time went by fast.

A book was assigned to her to study in between physical trials. It was filled with the codes being used and assured new codes would be supplied every so often, went to parachute school, because the plane transporting them wouldn't land. They would be dropped. Everything was so intense, as soon as her head hit the pillow each night she was asleep. The training was also exciting. Getting up early in the morning was no problem for her. She looked forward to what the day would bring.

Finally, the man in charge came to her unit. "I'll be expecting you right here tomorrow at midnight," he said. "You'll be leaving then. So it will still be dark when you jump back into Poland."

It was early in the morning on the last day, before she was to leave the training camp. Not having gone to bed, she dressed quickly. The parachute jump into Poland made her the most nervous. It was the most fearful part of the training. Jumping out of a plane and into a field where there might be Nazis scared her. But it was safer then driving into areas with the enemy all around. It had to be done so she could start her work with the resistance workers. Lily laid out her work clothes and packed her dressy ones into a small pack given to her in training. When she finished dressing and applying her makeup, the only thing she allowed herself to keep in her jacket pocket, she walked to the main tent and the officer in charge of the camp.

"You're early, but that's good. Pierre will be here any minute. I have some things for you."

The head of the training group gave her forged identity papers, a ration card, a map of the area where she would be dropped, and Polish Slots. It surprised her when the officer slipped a cyanide pill into a lipstick tube. *I hope I won't need that.*

"You should have a good jump. There will be a full moon and you will be landing in a farmer's open field."

"That's good. Jumping out of an airplane was the least likable thing about my training."

Pierre walked into the office just as Lily appeared with her belongings. "I'm glad you're ready early. I have a stop to make before we go to the plane."

CHAPTER SEVEN

January 1943

"We won't be long. It's still early. We have time."

"Where are we going?"

"You'll see. You're going to meet a very important man."

"I'm not dressed for the event."

"Don't worry. He knows you're with the Polish resistance. He's not interested in how you look. Driver stop."

"It looks like ordinary offices."

"It's war rooms. They have installed broadcasting and communication equipment. It's reinforced and soundproofed. This is the place where the staff of the armed forces and the government cabinet meet. They make all their military decisions here."

"I'm very interested."

"The two most important rooms are the map room and the cabinet room."

Lily peeked into the map room as they passed. "There are people in there."

"It's used twenty-four hours a day by officers from the Royal Airforce, the British Army, and the Royal Navy. The officers track the movements of all the troops throughout Europe. It's the center of all their military decisions. They prepare the daily intelligence reports for the King, the Prime Minister, and the military Chiefs of Staff. Mr. Churchill, the Prime Minister, directs the war from here. When the bombing, or the Blitz as the British call it, started they were protected by a gigantic piece of concrete or as they called it the slab. The slab covered the rooms. The individuals running the war stay here at night, though I suspect Mr. Churchill goes to his house around the corner at number 10 Downing Street."

"Pierre." Lily heard a booming voice call.

"Prime Minister," Pierre answered. "I came to pick up the maps."

"And who is this?" Churchill asked.

"This is Lily O'Malley, my American friend. She has just finished training at the camp outside London."

"Hello, Lily."

She smiled at the man who looked much like a bulldog, smoked a cigar, and spoke with a slight lisp. He seemed full of energy. The history books said that he inspired the British, uplifted the spirits, and his inspiration helped English people and the troops.

"I have the maps you need Pierre. I'll send all the changes as they happen."

"Thank you, Prime Minister."

"All right, get to your plane. It was nice to meet you, young lady." He lifted his glass of cognac in a salute.

"You also." She extended her hand. Churchill reached out and shook it with a strong grip. *Rachel will never believe this. I met Winston Churchill and shook his hand.*

Pierre took her hand and walked to the car.

"I'm happy you met him. He's had a mild heart attack. Hopefully, the stress of the war will not take a great man from us."

"I am too."

"We're going back to the same field we arrived at when we landed in England. It will be the same plane. There will be others with us. Some of them you trained with."

"I really didn't get to know anyone. The only things we did were train and sleep in our off time."

"Sorry, it was so intense. As I told you, with the war expanding all over Europe, we've had to speed up the training. You'll be with a lot of experienced fighters. They will help you."

"Looks like we're ready to board the plane." Lily followed Pierre as he walked up steps.

Big Ben, the bell clock at the Palace of Westminster in London, chimed as she waited for the plane to take off. She hummed along with the music from Handel's Messiah coming from the bells.

There were two women and four men who would be jumping to the drop zone in the Midnight Sonata mission, the name given to these missions because they were at night. The plane roared its motor and the propellers spun as they taxied on the runway. It took off smoothly without problems. Lily smiled. *No muddy field this time.* "Where are the men we came with?" she asked Pierre.

"They are staying a little longer. The people on this flight have finished their training."

"I don't remember seeing them while I trained."

"There are many groups. You probably will never see the same people twice."

"We're almost there." She heard a whisper in her ear. "About fifteen minutes away."

Looking up, she saw Pierre and felt him give her a little shake as he spoke.

"I wasn't really asleep. Just resting my eyes and thinking about what is to come." Her eyebrows were furrowed. Lily fought the cobwebs of sleep.

"We're at 10,000 feet so it will be an easy jump. Look out the window there is a cloud cover so we'll be hidden."

Lily waited as the plane flew for short time.

"It's almost time."

"I hope the Germans are not waiting for us," she murmured as she stared at the full moon. "The clouds have cleared. See the full moon."

"Don't worry, so far, I've heard they still haven't found any of our landing places."

Pierre put his arm around her shoulder and hugged her gently. "Okay, it's time to get in line. I'll be right behind you. You have nothing to worry about."

The adrenaline began to build as Lily watched while the other woman and the men made their jumps. Awkwardly, she cleared her throat as she stood at the edge of the open door facing the plane, moved her body away from the plane, released her hands, and pushed away with her feet. A soft gasp escaped her lips. Her arms and legs stuck out like a bird. The rush of the wind excited her as she soared through the air. The wind noise was loud in her ears. It was more fun than in training. The tense lines in her forehead began to relax.

When she thought she was at about thirty feet above the ground she moved her hand to the lever and tugged. Hearing a loud popping noise, she looked up to make sure the chute opened. *It did. I'll be okay.* She reached for the brake and pulled on it to slow down the descent. When she hit the ground with a thud, knocking the wind out of her, she laid stunned.

"Are you all right?" Pierre asked as he landed and rushed to her side.

She bit down hard on her lower lip laying very still as she took a minute to catch her breath... "I'm fine. My breath is back. I forgot to bend my knees so I would have a soft landing." Standing up she unclipped the parachute. A group of men ran from the woods and began to grab the chutes. Relieved when she realized they were friendly, she smiled "The ground is hard now. At least I didn't land in mud."

"Come on," Pierre called out to the others. "Let's go. We need to get out of here fast. Even if the Germans don't know about this area we don't want to take any chances."

"What happens to the chutes?" Lily asked as they hiked toward the woods.

"The farmers will repack and hide them until we need to use them again." Pierre grabbed her hand and ran, pulling her to the woods.

"Where are we going?" she asked hearing the plane leave the area. She listened for shots from guns. Not hearing any she sighed with relief. *We are safe.*

"Our first stop is the farmer living near here. It will only take five or ten minutes to get there if we walk fast." He smiled. "It's dark but we still have to be careful. You people stay in the woods," he said to the Partisans walking with them. "Don't come out of the trees until I signal you."

As they reached the wooded area near the barn, Lily saw the farmer running toward them. "The Germans are in the house. You have to hide in the barn. Get under the hay because sometimes they go there and take a horse or some piece of equipment they need."

"They may see us if we go in the front door," Pierre said.

"There's a small trap door at the back of the barn. You'll have to crawl through it. Climb to the loft and cover yourselves with hay."

Lily ran keeping up with Pierre as they made their way to the back door. "Here it is." She bent down, and inched her fingers in what looked like a slit in the lower back wall of the barn and pulled. The door opened.

"Follow me, I want to make sure no one is sitting in there," Pierre said, as he pushed ahead of her and crawled through.

A faint thread of hysteria entered her mind as she watched Pierre shove his broad shoulders from side to side pushing into the barn.

Looking out of the window in the horse stall he pulled on her arm. "Hurry. The front door of the house opened." He followed her up the ladder. "They're outside and coming toward the barn. Cover up," he whispered as he peeked around the side of the loft's open door. He laid down and covered himself.

After she covered herself, Lily pushed a little of the hay away from one eye and peeked out when she heard the barn door open. One of the soldiers who was smoking threw his lit cigarette on the barn floor. The hay didn't ignite, but she waited for smoke. Not seeing any she felt relief. *Thank goodness he ground it out with the toe of his boot. I'd hate to try to escape a fire with German soldiers hanging around in the yard. He's picked up a wagon wheel.*

"They're leaving," she murmured. When one of the soldiers slid the door to close it, she waited until she heard it slam shut then scrambled down the ladder behind Pierre.

"Let's get to the house and see if we can get some supplies." He slid the door open a crack and peeked out. "They're on the road driving away from the house. Come on." Pierre grabbed her hand pulling her to the house.

Lily ran up the front porch steps and knocked on the door. Someone peeked out the window next to the entrance.

"Hurry. Come in," the farmer said as he opened the door and yanked her and Pierre into the house. "Guns, grenades, and knives were dropped last night. I have them hidden under the floor boards. Stay here, I'll get them." The farmer hurried to the back of the house.

Pierre walked out the front door and waved toward the forest.

Lily followed, stretched her head around him, and saw the people who were on the plane running toward the house. They stopped at the end of the sidewalk and waited.

As she stood with Pierre on the last step of the porch, the old man returned with a bag of weapons. Lily heard him whisper to Pierre, "Weapons from the drop the day before your jump."

"Do you have some food?" Pierre asked turning toward the old man.

"I have some bread, cheese, and sausages. You can have them. Wait. I'll put them in a sack."

When he returned, Lily reached out her hand and took the bag the man handed to her. Pulling the string, closing the burlap bag, she slung it over her shoulder.

Following Pierre, she met the others when they reached the end of the farmer's property.

The leaves crunched under her feet as they moved deep into the woods. "What's the first thing on the agenda?"

"We have to build a *zemlyanka*, dugout."

"What kind of weapons did the farmer give you?"

"Some machine and hand guns, grenades, TNT and other things to blow up trains and buildings. We'll collect other weapons as we move around."

"Are we meeting the others we left when we went to England?"

"Yes. They've been sabotaging vital German war machines and started to dig another hut. We'll stay in it while we make more plans."

"Finally, a rest." Lily smiled.

Lily looked at the hut when they reached the group. "Good, it looks as if they're almost finished. Why is a barn door on the floor?"

"I hope they didn't steal the door from one of the farmers that have been good to us."

"What's a door for?"

"We use it for the floor so we're not sitting on cold dirt. It takes a while to make the hideout because they have to carry the dirt far from the hut in case the Germans do come into the woods. They have been working very hard."

"You're right, Pierre. We started early this morning." One of the young men smiled as he dug his shovel into the dirt. "We're finished. Now, we better get ready with TNT and grenades. A farmer told me there will be a convoy of Germans coming on the road close to here."

She watched the Partisans cut limbs from the pine trees nearby and cover the shelter.

Well, that's done. It's not a great place to sleep, but it's better than a bunk in a prison camp or an open field.

"Are we safe?"

"Yes."

"Shall we break out what's in the bag the farmer gave us?" Lily asked.

"Yes. It's starting to get light. We'll have some food then get to the road and wait for the convoy."

"They will get an early morning surprise." Lily took the last sip of wine, slung a rifle strap over her shoulder, and stuffed her pockets with grenades and bullets. "I'm ready." She waited as Pierre pulled something from a bag and tuck it under some of the branches.

"Here's an armband." He tossed her a white band with a red circle. "This will identify you as a Polish Partisan. So you won't get shot by your own men."

"I think I'll stay outside and keep watch until it's time to go."

Lily stared up at the gray sky. "I'll keep you company."

The gray sky turned into dawn as Pierre gathered the men and women together. The band tied around her arm made her feel safe. She trailed the group, running behind them to the location of the mission. When the group stopped, hiding under the cover of the bushes on the side of the road made her feel safe, but her relief was short-lived. As the rumble of tanks and the roar of the jeep motors got closer to her hiding place, her heart jumped in her chest. She pulled a grenade from her pocket and paid attention to Pierre as he raised his hand lifting one, two, three fingers then brought his hand down. Lily pulled the pin and tossed it.

The soldiers jumped from their tanks and cars. They shot their guns into the bushes. Pulling another grenade from her pocket, she repeated what she had just done. Her breath cut off as she saw a soldier come toward her. She could feel her face turn cold. Icy fear twisted around her heart. Fear knotted inside her. Slipping her rifle off her shoulder, she pointed it at him. When he was close enough, she pulled the trigger and shot. Watching his face freeze, she saw blood run down his cheek. Lily jumped back and her body stiffened as he fell at her feet.

"Grab their guns and jackets. We'll need the jackets. The weather is getting colder."

Lily cringed as she stripped the soldiers of their jackets. After she made sure the soldier who fell at her feet was dead, she sighed. Pulling off his shoes, she stared at his socks. *Wool, that'll keep someone's feet warm.* She tugged off more shoes as quickly as she could, removed socks, and stuffed them into her pockets.

"Stay down."

"What is it, Pierre?" she asked as she turned and saw his gun pointed in her direction.

Lily heard the hiss of a bullet from Pierre's gun as it whizzed past her head. "What? What are you doing?"

"One of the soldiers was still alive and just about ready to shoot you. Come on. Let's get out of here. Back to the dugout."

She crawled into the *zemlyanka* and sat, leaning against the dirt wall. She put the soldier's jacket over her shoulders and shivered. Wearing the jacket of the man she just killed, made her shudder, but he didn't need it and she felt warmer. The hut was empty except for a wine bottle sitting in the corner. She checked. It wasn't empty. She put it to her mouth and drained it. Taking a deep breath, she tried to relax. Little by little warmth crept back into her body. Sitting in silence, she smiled when Pierre crawled in and sat down beside her.

"What's our next assignment?"

"I have to radio SOE in London and find out the next target. I'll be right back. It will only take a minute. I don't like to stay on the radio too long so they can't trace us. The Germans are always listening and tracking." He left the dugout and walked toward the road.

Lily closed her eyes and waited.

"Okay. Got it." He carried a map in his hand when he sat down in the hut.

Lily opened her eyes and smiled. She was beginning to get a second wind and starting to feel excited. "Where's the radio?"

"In my backpack. We're going to hit a munitions factory and sabotage a power plant." He opened the map. "We're close to the factory. It's just three miles through the woods."

"When are we going to leave?"

"Soon. We'll stop at another farmhouse on the way and hide there until dark. The factory is only a mile from the farmhouse. The Germans take most of the food from the families, but hopefully, they'll have enough to give us some."

"Where's the power plant?"

"In the next town. With any luck, the Germans will be so busy trying to stop the fire and wreckage of the factory they won't be paying attention to anything else. We'll be able to hit the power plant and get back to our hiding place without any trouble. We'll cut the phone lines on our way to the plant, just in case they try to contact soldiers from other areas to help them."

Lily sat at the door of the hut. "What can I do to help?"

"Load up your backpack with dynamite, blasting caps, wicks, and detonation cord. The boys will help you. The things you need are in the box next to the hut under pine branches."

Lily followed his instructions stuffing the equipment she would need to blow up the buildings into her backpack. She sat and waited.

"All right, we're ready. Let's go," Pierre yelled. "Come on, Lily." He stuck out his hand and pulled her out of the hut to a standing position.

Reaching into the box, she removed what she needed.

"Got everything?"

"Yes." Hurrying to his side, she walked through the heaviest part of the trees.

As she walked, she saw one of the boys approach Pierre and pull him to the side.

"What's wrong with him? He looks worried," she asked when the boy went back to the group.

"He was worried about the farmer," Pierre said. We have to be very careful who we use. Some of the people are Nazi sympathizers. They pretend to be a friend and will turn you in for a bag of sugar or a bottle of vodka. I told him the farmer has been checked out."

"He didn't seem very relieved after he talked to you."

"It's hard to convince them sometimes. Here we are." He raised his arm and motioned the party to go into the barn.

"Get into the barn," Pierre said. "If you hear a car or tanks hide, hide under the hay. I'm going to the farmhouse. Lily, come with me."

Lily walked along with Pierre. As she reached the front yard of the house, she saw a man riding up to the porch on a bike. He waved to Pierre and parked the cycle as he slid off the rubber covering the right handlebar and pulled out a piece of paper from the opening. He handed it to Pierre.

"That's a great trick. Putting messages in bike handlebars is better than sending them by radio and getting caught."

"Thanks," Pierre said to the man and then smiled as he read.

"Why are you so pleased?"

"Seems as if there will be a skeleton crew at the factory tonight, because there is another speech by Hitler. As usual, all the soldiers will be at the camp to listen to the message. The back of the building is not being watched as carefully as usual by guards."

"That means we'll have more time to plant the explosives. He also said a wagon will be coming with the usual milk barrels."

"Usual milk barrels?"

"Yes, they pour out the milk and transport guns and ammunition in the empty barrels."

"Little did the Germans know when they appropriated the gasoline and cars that espionage could still be accomplished. The Partisans are still getting messages through," Pierre said. "The farmer also said his wife is setting up a dinner for us. Let's get the others. When we finish, it will be time to go." He called to the rest of the crew. They came running, reaching the table before she did.

Lily finished her last bite of pie and emptied her coffee cup. "Dinner was wonderful," she said to the farmer's wife.

"Time to go," Pierre called to the group as he motioned them to follow. "Grab your packs and let's go. Lily, you'll work with Jacek." He pointed to the young man that gave her some of his clothes.

She smiled as she picked up her backpack and walked beside Jacek. Surprised flitted through her when they reached the factory before she knew it. *I guess we were all running on adrenaline. It's taken so little time to get here.*

They approached the factory but waited in the woods until Pierre signaled them to leave. When they reached the side of the building, Pierre raised his hand for them to wait.

Lily watched him walk toward their target. He suddenly flattened himself against the wall of the building as a soldier turned the corner. He stood in front of Pierre. Her stomach felt as if it fell to her knees. Her body stiffened as Pierre pointed his gun, grabbed the soldier around the neck, and the man fell. She sighed with relief when Pierre dragged him behind a bush.

"Come on." Jacek pulled her out of the woods. "We're on our way to the first floor, Pierre," Jacek said as Pierre ran up the outdoor stairs and entered the building on the second floor.

Lily threw open the back door and entered.

Jacek pulled on her arm. He raised his finger to his lips. "Ssssh, ssssh. Get behind that stack of boxes," he whispered.

Lily immediately moved behind the pile of cartons and held her breath as a soldier walked into the open room. She inhaled deeply and released the breath when he looked around, turned, and left the room as rapidly as he arrived.

"Get all the stuff out of the pack. We're going to make a slow motion explosion. All right, Lily, take this detonation cord, attach blasting caps, and TNT at intervals. Pierre is on another floor doing the same thing we're doing. The detonation cord is soaked in compressed nitroglycerin powder and covered with waterproof plastic. It detonates at four miles per second. We'll leave long spaces between the sticks of TNT."

Lily watched and followed the same procedure as Jacek. Relieved when she heard no footsteps, she worked quickly as she laid the explosives on the other side of the room.

They finished uncoiling the wire at the stairs leading to the second floor. Lily looked up when she heard footsteps. "Oh no." Her heart beat jumped in her chest as she looked around for a place to hide. Looking up again, she whispered. "It's Pierre." A soft gasp of relief escaped her as she watched him walking beside one of the Partisans who was running a coil as he moved down the steps to the first floor.

"Come on. Light the end of the cord and run. Run as fast as you can."

Lily reached the woods just as the building exploded. She threw herself on the ground and covered her ears. When the explosions stopped, she watched the fire that was caused by the explosives and the ammunition the Germans stored in the building. The soldiers left to guard the building tried to put it out. Finally, they gave up, ran to their jeeps, and drove toward the camp.

"Where are the rest of the crew?"

"They're cutting phone lines. We have to get to the power plant. They'll join us there. We're going to do the same thing we did at the factory."

Lily looked up as she stood at the edge of the woods. She saw headlights stab the darkness. "Get back. There are Germans on the road. Stay in the woods."

CHAPTER EIGHT

February 1943

It was early morning when the group reached the farmhouse.

Lily laid back on the bale of hay on the barn floor. She was drained.

"Are you all right?" Pierre asked.

"I'm fine. I just need to rest for a few minutes."

"The farmer's wife will feed us before we head back to the dugout."

"What about the Germans?" Lily closed her eyes.

"They're busy putting out the fires and won't bother any of the locals."

After a few minutes, Lily sat up. "I smell coffee." She strolled to the farmhouse with the other Partisans. "Just what I need, food." The stack of pancakes and sausage patties the woman set in front of her made her smile. "We haven't eaten since yesterday. The food looks so good," she said as she spread the pancakes with fresh butter and spooned some syrup over them. No words were uttered until her plate was empty.

"Everybody finished? Ready? Time to get back to camp, people," Pierre said as he moved to the doorway. "Thank you for your hospitality." Carrying a burlap bag, he nodded to the farmer and his wife.

Lily hugged them both before she left the kitchen and followed the group. She looked up at the bright sun. "We'll get back just in time for dinner. I assume the farmer gave you some food?"

"Yes. Cheeses, fruit, bread, and a couple bottles of wine."

"Good. All this exercise and excitement gives me a hearty appetite."

"We're almost at the dugout, Lily. Some of the group is writing about our escapades and will distribute it to the underground paper when we get back to Warsaw. It prints the Partisan's and escaped prisoner's stories and distributes to the people. It's good for everyone to see our accomplishments and how we are helping to defeat the enemy. It helps us get new members."

"I see our camp." She dashed to a tree near the entrance of the dugout and plopped down in front of it.

"I'm going to get on the radio."

"Wait."

"What is it?"

Lily put her finger to her lips. "Shush, shush. Do you hear that?'

"What?"

"It sounds like a child crying."

"Maybe it's a cat."

"No. It's a child." Lily stood up and listened. Quietly walking around the bushes behind her, she stared. "Here they are." She reached down and pulled a small boy and girl from the shrubs. "Where did you come from?"

The little boy looked at his sister. "Don't talk to them. They may be bad people."

"We won't hurt you." Lily watched the little girl begin to cry. "It's all right. We won't hurt you." The boy reach out and held the girl's hand. A tear ran down his cheek.

"Where are your parents?" Lily knelt down and put her arm around the little girl. "It's all right. "How old are you?"

"I'm five and my sister is three. I take care of her." The boy tried to pull his sister away from Lily.

"Yes, you do. You are doing a good job. Where do you live?"

"We live in a house. It's over there on the road."

He pointed through the woods. Our parents hid us when they heard the soldiers coming. They were taken away by soldiers. We left when we thought the soldiers were gone."

"I'm Lily and this is Pierre. What are your names?"

"I'm Abraham and my sister's name is Hanna."

"I'm hungry," the little girl whined.

"Pierre, give them some of the bread and cheese."

"We have an Abraham that works with us he's not here right now, but he'll be here soon," Pierre said.

She watched them as they ate. They barely chewed a piece of food before they stuffed more into their mouths. "How long has it been since you ate?"

"We had breakfast yesterday."

"Eat all you want. Are you warm enough?"

"Pierre, do you think we could take them to the nuns at the convent in Warsaw? They help get children and families out of Poland."

"We can do that tonight."

"Are you full now?" Lily asked.

The children nodded and smiled. They stood next to Lily. Hanna held on to her leg.

Lily looked at the ground. She gathered up grass and sticks and decorated the fingers of her knitted gloves. Sitting down, she leaned against a tree to make hair out of grass, arms and legs from sticks, and clothes by threading the materials she found on the ground into the wool.

Leading the children to the open entrance of the hut she said, "Come into the hut and sit down next to me. I want to tell you some stories. The children curled up next to her as she began to make her finger puppets talk. She told the stories, using different voices and wiggling her fingers. The little girl laughed at the story of the three little pigs. Both of them listened when she began to tell the story of Hansel and Gretel. Soon she heard them breathing evenly and quietly. When she looked down, they were fast asleep.

"Please, Pierre, hand me that jacket in the pocket of my backpack. It's a German coat. I hope it won't scare them when they wake up, but it's heavy and will keep them warm. I know the nuns will help us with the children." She smiled, covered the children, and crawled from the hut.

"I need to make contact with some of the Partisans in Warsaw. While I'm doing that you can meet with the Mother Superior."

Lily leaned against the tree and sipped a glass of red wine. As she began to drift to sleep, Lily felt Pierre take her glass from her hand.

Lily opened her eye as the moonlight fell on her face. "Children, wake up we're going to leave here and take you to a safer place." Lily smiled. "Okay, guys." She looked at the Partisans. "These children need to be carried on your shoulders. We're going to the convent in Warsaw, but first, we're going to stop at their house." Lily began to hum an American children's song as they walked through the woods. "A B C..."

The woods hid them from the road as they walked. When she saw a small house near the edge of the road and in front of her she pointed across the street. "Is that your house?"

"Yes." The little boy said. "That's our house."

"Ma," the little girl cried scrambled off the Partisans shoulder and ran crossing the street she ran up the steps to the front door and stood very still.

"Ma and Da are gone. She doesn't understand we are alone," her brother said to Lily.

He is so grown up for his age, Lily thought.

"Will they be at the nuns," the girl cried.

"We'll never see them again," he said to his sister. His face showed no expression.

Lily heard Hanna begin to cry. "It's okay, we'll find good people for you to be with until we find your parents." The little girl wrapped her arms around Lily's thighs. Lily picked her up.

She threw open the door. "Anybody here?" No one answered. Looking around as she carried Hanna into the front hall, she stopped and waited for Pierre and the others to join her.

"Let me get some clothes from the house. Wait, it will only take a minute."

Lily put the little girl down and took her hand. "Jacek, can you help?"

"Sure." He followed.

"Hanna. Show me where your room is."

The little girl pointed to the staircase at the back of the house.

Lily entered the front door and walked up the stairs to the little girl's room.

"It's all the way in the back." The girl pointed to the last room.

Lily threw enough clothes in her backpack to last several days.

"I want my teddy bear," the girl cried.

Lily looked around the room. "All right here he is." Lily picked the toy bear off the floor near her bed and watched the little girl clutch it to her chest.

"Abraham, show me where your room is." Lily piled his clothes in her arms. "They don't fit in my pack. Can you take them, Jacek?" she asked as she checked to make sure everything was stuffed into his pack.

"Let's go. We have some warm clothes and a few toys," Lily said to Pierre. "It's starting to get cold now." She took out the sweaters she packed and helped the girl put hers on. "Jacek, give Abraham his sweater, please," she said as she handed the little boys sweater to Jacek.

They walked all day through the woods. It was dusk when they reached the woods near the convent.

"We have to wait until it's dark to go into the convent so we're not seen. The convent is watched during the daylight and sometimes at night but it is easier to sneak in through the back entrance at night," Pierre said. "We'll just wait at the edge of the woods."

"Oh, no. There's a soldier marching around the yard. What are we going to do?"

"It looks as if there is only one soldier. I'll take care of him. As soon as it's done, run. Run as fast as you can and knock at the door. Two short knocks stop then three more knocks."

Lily watched Pierre sneak up behind the soldier and grab him around the neck. When the soldier dropped, he pulled him into the woods.

I wonder if breaking his neck is how he killed the soldier at the factory. She shivered even though she was getting used to seeing someone murdered so the group would be safe.

She grabbed the children's hands and ran, pulling them along with her. Reaching the convent back door, she knocked with the code. When the door opened, she gently pushed the children into the convent. "We're here." Kneeling down so her face was on the same level as theirs, she whispered, "It's going to be all right. This lady will help you. She is very kind and has helped many children like you."

"Mother Superior, I have two new children for you. We found them in the woods. They hid there when their parents were taken away by the Nazis."

Lily heard someone running down the hallway to the door. Her friend, Rachel, flew into her arms.

"Lily, I thought I'd lost you." Rachel cried out. "What have you been doing?"

"You know I went to England. I had some training in espionage. I hoped I would see you when I got back to Poland. Have you been helping escapees?"

"Yes. I wanted to stay and help at the convent."

"If we ever get back to the twenty-first century, we'll be able to say we helped save some of the Jews from execution in Poland death camps," Rachel whispered as she leaned toward Lily's ear. Rachel smiled. "I'm working with the nuns to helped Jewish children flee from the Nazis."

Lily heard the coded knock at the door. "It's the Partisans." She watched the nun open the door.

"We had to hide the body so the sisters won't get into trouble," Jacek said.

"All right, sister, get the children to bed in the bell tower," Mother Superior said to the young nun who entered the room.

"Tomorrow we're taking a group of children to Sweden. You're welcome to come with us," the Mother Superior said turning to Lily and Pierre.

"I think Lily can go with you. I'll stay with the group of Partisans and make mischief for the Germans. Can you add these two children to the group?" Pierre smiled.

"Of course. They're little. We'll add them to the group. We have room," the nun said.

"We have to leave now. I'll see you when you get back, Lily." He gave her a hug and hurried from the convent.

The nun shut the door after the group left. "All right, Rachel, show Lily her bed, please. We have an early start in the morning, Lily, right after midnight. It has to be dark so the Germans can't examine the wagon if we meet them on the road. It's cold so they don't usually stop us. They want to get to their barracks and warmth."

"All right, ladies. It's time to get ready to leave," the Mother Superior called out as she climbed the stairs of the bell tower. She knocked on the door of their hiding place. "Hurry."

"We're awake," Lily called back. The small cracks in the walls of the room let in the moonlight. "It's still dark and time to go, Rachel."

"I'm going to stay here. I hope I can get back to our time. At least for a while. I miss Karl."

"Keep watch on everything that happens. I'll see you when I get back." Lily smiled. "I guess one of the nuns is going to travel with me and the children."

"Is everybody ready?" Lily asked as she walked toward the wagon she saw in the barn. "Where are the children?"

"The children are in the wagon in the barrels. We tell anybody that stops us we are picking up fish and other supplies from the seaport. We tell the Germans we need the barrels to do this. Because it's dark and if we're stopped by the soldiers, they can't see the air holes drilled in the barrels. We have fooled them so far." She smiled. "I have a sweater, Habit and cornette for you to wear Lily. Also, take this blanket. These nights are cold."

"Wait." Lily took the clothes. Holding them, she asked the nun some questions about the passengers.

"Where were the children?"

"We hid them in the convent and homes near us. We've brought the ones that are going to Sweden to the convent yesterday."

"How many children will be going?" Lily set the clothes from the abbess on the chair next to her.

"We take eight. We've added your two, so there will be ten."

"The Danish fishing boats that go to Swedish waters are only thirty-seven feet long, fourteen feet wide, and six feet deep so we usually only take eight and the two of us. We make about two trips a week. I'm sending the sister who usually goes with me on this trip. She'll show you how things work. You'll be taking my place."

"I'll be back soon, Rachel. Take care," Lily said slipping on one of the nun's clothes Mother Superior had handed to her. She grabbed a blanket and headed to the gate. "See you soon," she threw the words over her shoulder. Waving to her friend and the nuns standing in the doorway of the convent, she jumped onto the wagon as the sister slowed up when she drove toward her.

"Do you take adults?" Lily asked as they drove to the road outside the convent.

"We usually take families, children and their parents over the Tatra Mountains and get them to Switzerland. Children are the only people we have now, but adults will come and stay at the convent soon. We have a scheduled mountain trip in about a week. We try to keep families together. These children, the ones we take in the barrels, are alone. Their parents have disappeared. We bring them to new families in neutral Sweden."

"How old are the children?"

"They are five years old to fifteen years."

"How long will the trip take, sister?"

"We won't get there until early tomorrow morning around one or two. So about twenty-four hours. We'll stop when it gets light at a farmer's house, let the children out of their hiding places to stretch and feed them. When it gets dark again, we'll load our cargo and travel again. The soldier, who patrol the docks are less diligent at that time and that's when the fishing boats motor out to the Baltic Sea to fish."

"That's a long time for little children and even a fifteen-year-old to be curled up in a barrel."

"You're right, but they are so undernourished from living in a Ghetto or prison camp they are small for their ages."

"Do you ever meet soldiers on the road when you travel?" Lily shivered with the thought of meeting Germans on their trip.

"Sometimes."

"Do they stop you?"

"Usually."

"What do you tell them?"

Since we're following the Vistula River, if they see and stop us, we tell them we're going to the port to bring back fish and food for the people and the troops. So far they have not stopped us and searched the wagon. On the way back, they grab a lot of the food if they meet us. They let us go." The nun whipped the horses. "Stealing from us makes them feel important. After they steal from us, they can brag they got food to share with their troops."

"Be careful. Here comes a car full of soldiers. The driver is coming right toward us. They have frightened the horses." She pulled on the reins to slow the horses. "Quick. Cover up your feet with the blanket. Nuns don't wear ankle boots. Hurry. Hurry. Don't speak."

"Oh." Lily grabbed the blanket, leaned down and covered her feet and lap. A soft gasp escaped her when the car rolled toward them. He blocked the wagon so the nun couldn't go anywhere.

The sister pulled on the reins again, lurching backward as the team suddenly stopped. The horses reared up on their back legs, their front legs in the air.

"Halt," the passenger, an officer, of the jeep yelled to the driver as he stood up. The jeep kept rolling closer to the nun's wagon. "Soldier. Halt. You're going to run into the wagon and damage the jeep."

The officer staggered backward as the driver pushed his foot down and slammed on his breaks.

"Hans. Be careful, you dolt." He clutched the frame of the front window of the jeep. "Halt. Sisters, halt."

As the nun grabbed onto the reins and pulled, calming the horses down, Lily bent down making sure the blanket was tucked around her boots.

"What are you sisters doing? Why are you on the road at night? Why are you in such a hurry?" he demanded.

"You must be new. We make this trip twice a week. We're going to Gdansk to pick up fish from the fishermen and food from some of the local farmers. We have to meet the fishing boat before they go out to sea. We load our barrels on their boats so the fisherman can fill them. We're running late."

"What's in the barrels?"

"They are empty. The food and fish we're picking up will go in them."

"And what about you, Sister?" He pointed to Lily with the crop he held in his hand.

No words left her lips. Her eyes widened in astonishment. She flinched when the end of the crop he held in his hand came down and hit her shoulder.

"Sister, answer me?" he yelled. "What's wrong? Doesn't she speak? Answer me." He poked Lily again with the riding crop.

Lily closed her eyes quickly as they met the officer's cold ones. Eyes that were hooded like a shark's. A shock ran through her. A breath caught in her lungs. Fright swept through her. Her pulse beat erratically. Panic like she had never felt before welled in her throat.

"This one is deaf and only understands hand signals." The nun signed to Lily. Pretend you are cold, the nun leaned toward Lily and whispered.

Lily pulled her coat close to her.

"Another defective person we should get rid of." A shadow of annoyance crossed his face. His tongue was heavy with sarcasm. His hard glare burned through her as he started to step over the side of the jeep acting as if he was going to walk toward her.

Lily pulled the blanket up around her shoulders and feigned a shiver.

"All right, never mind. Get going. Bring us some good fish." He turned and pointed his finger forward after he sat back into his seat. "Go, Hans. These nuns can be trouble, but they bring us some good food."

Lily looked down at the floorboard of the wagon. The driver revved the motor of the jeep getting her attention again.

"Heil Hitler." He raised his arm in a salute. The driver drove away as quickly as he had stopped, not waiting until the nuns returned his salute.

As the wagon bumped down the road. Lily turned her head and looked over her shoulder. The tail lights of the jeep had disappeared.

"How much longer until we reach the farm?" Lily asked.

"We'll be there in about ten minutes."

"It's starting to get light. The sun will be bright before we know it. From the farmer's house, we'll have about five or six hours to the port. We'll leave as soon as it gets dark. The fishermen will load the barrels quickly so we can get out to the Baltic Sea and on our way to Sweden and neutral territory when the sun comes up again."

When they reached the farmer's house, Lily smiled as they drove the wagon into the barn next to a sprawling farm house.

"Let the children out of the barrels. They are nailed down so you have to pry them open."

"Children into the house," Lily said as they scrambled from the barrels and wagon. Go to the lady in the doorway." She pointed toward the heavy set woman opening the door of the house. "Run."

"Come in. Come in. Hurry before someone sees you." Wiping her hands on her flowered apron, she brushed a wisp of hair from her cheek and tucked it into a knot at the back of her neck.

Lily ran along with them to the house. A meal was set out on the table. It was so filled with food there was hardly room enough for plates. The children stared at the meat, vegetables, and bread and butter, and milk. They rushed to the benches on either side of the kitchen table and sat. Barely chewing the food before they swallowed, they ate as if they would never eat again. *What appetites. Let's hope we get to our destination so they finally get enough food every day and a safe place to stay until this holocaust is over.*

After dinner, the children played together in the barn with the farmer's dog.

"Did you have a dog?" she asked Abraham.

"Yes. He ran away when the soldiers came."

"Maybe you can have one when you get to Sweden."

He smiled. "I would name him Boy. My dog's name was Boy. No one will take him away there. Will they?"

"No. Sweden is going to be a very nice place and a very safe place," Lily said.

"Come on, children, it's time to take a nap," the nun called.

When they laid down in the hay Lily covered them with blankets hanging in the barn. She sat next to the group and sang them a lullaby. Soon they were all asleep. With her back against the barn wall, she thought about her trip to Poland and what had been happening to her.

After a couple of hours, she saw the nun come into the barn and motioned to her. Brushing the bits of hay stuck to her clothes as she stood, she woke the children and helped the nun lead the children to the wagon and into the barrels. They covered the children with blankets before they climbed into their hiding place. The lids were the last thing to go on the barrels.

"We have to be very careful. A group of jeeps and trucks with Nazi soldiers went by the house while we waited for dark. Did you hear them?"

"I thought I heard something, I was deep in thought. When they went by and didn't stop, I decided I was dreaming."

"We're ready. Get into your seat, Lily."

The farmer and his wife stood by the wagon and hugged the nun and Lily.

"Thank you very much, "Lily said.

"Have a safe and good trip," they called as the nun drove the wagon out of the yard and onto the road.

Lily looked out over the Vistula River as they drove next to it while they traveled to the coastline. "The river is frozen."

"Yes, it freezes in the winter. The Nazis use prisoners to cut blocks of ice from the river, the blocks are sent by trucks to beer houses in the cities. No warm beer for the Germans. Even if some of the prisoners die when they fall into the water."

Lily leaned back against the seat and quietly watched the houses of the small villages as they passed through the quiet countryside. There were no lights shining from inside the houses. *The residents are asleep and safe for now. They don't know what's coming and wouldn't believe it if I told them.*

Finally, she saw the bright lights of the docks. The fishermen were busily loading nets and gear on the fleet of boats at the dock in the harbor. She could see the outline of large sand dunes at the end of the dock. Seagrass grew in spots on them and pieces of wood sat at the bottom of the sandbanks.

CHAPTER NINE

"We're here," the nun called to the children. Lily heard them wiggle and cry out. "Shush. We're not in a safe place yet. There are soldiers close by. We have to be quiet just a little while longer. Once you get on the boat and we're out to sea, you can make as much noise as you want," the nun said.

Lily looked out over the Baltic Sea as they neared the dock. "The water is rough." The waves slapped at the dock and the boats bump into each other as high waves threw them around. Lily stared at the nun as she motioned to the fisherman who sat on the sea wall smoking and talking with another man. After the nun pulled the wagon near the dock, the fishermen threw their cigarettes into the water.

They jumped up, ran to the storage building, and pushed open its heavy doors. When the wagon stopped, they pulled the horses and it into the building. She watched them unload the barrels and set them next to the door. They slid the doors closed after the nun and Lily got out of the wagon, and began to load their boats with nets and fishing gear.

"When they finish loading the boats with their fishing needs, the children will be taken out of the barrels and led onto a boat and hidden. If the Germans check as the barrels are being loaded they will find only empty ones on the fishing boats. There are lots of soldiers around," the nun said. "We'll have to be very careful. We'll leave the children in the barrels until we're ready to go."

"Finally." Lily smiled. "We're almost at the end." She followed the fishermen as they went back into the building. When they finished, figuring how many barrels they had, they shut the door, went back to their boats, and continued their routine that needed to be completed before they went to sea.

Lily heard a knock at the door and ducked behind the barrels, peeked around them, and stared as the nun slid the door open just enough for the man who seemed to fit through with a little difficulty. The nun whispered, "Enter," then murmured something to him Lily was unable to hear. His eyes shifted from side to side as he handed the sister what looked like a pile of cards. The nun dug into the pocket of her habit and pushed something into his hand. He stuffed what the nun had pressed into his hand into his pocket and left as fast as he came.

Lily moved toward the nun. She watched her cram the cards in her habit. "What are those? What did he bring you?" Lily asked as the nun turned and closed the door quickly.

"Forged passports and papers identifying the children as Christians and Swedish citizens. They'll carry these from now on. The older children will be in charge of carrying them for the younger ones until their Swedish families take them.

"We'll be on our way shortly. The soldiers change shifts in about fifteen minutes. They meet at the guard house and start patrolling at the entrance of the docks. That's when we'll load the children onto the boat." The nun smiled. "The fishermen will help with the transfer. The boat we'll be escaping is not that far away. I'm sure they'll make it in a few seconds." The nun sighed. "I've left the tops of the barrels unnailed so we can lift the lids quickly, help the children out of the barrels, and run with them to the boat. With the help, it won't take long."

"Which boat will we sail on? I see several."

"The captain said the boat with the blue sails next to the pile of crates is the one we'll tell the children to get aboard. It's the first ship they'll come to when we reach the docked boats. It's a Danish boat. The children will be ferried secretly by small Swedish boats once we are in the neutral waters of Sweden. These boats will transfer them to a larger boat to the docks of Stockholm. Families will pick them up from there and begin to take care of them."

"Why Danish boats?"

"The Prime Minister, Per Albin Hansson, has worked out a deal with the Germans. They let the Danes trade with the Swedes even though the Germans occupy Denmark and Sweden is neutral. Frequently boats are run from Copenhagen to Stockholm. We use the same routine. So far no one thinks there's anything wrong if they see Danish boats making contact with Swedish ones."

The nun opened the door of the building and peeked out. "The soldiers have already walked to the front of the shipyard. They are on their way back so we have to hurry. They will be suspicious if the boats are not starting their motors soon. We have to make sure the fishermen's routine doesn't change." She stuck her hand out of the door and signaled to the fishermen standing around on the dock and smoking. "Okay, it's time," she called as she began to help the children out of the barrels.

Lily ran to the containers and helped. "Wait until everyone is out. Stay together." She motioned to the children to follow her and the nun.

The fishermen ran from the boat to the building, and each grabbed one of the hands of the children to lead them to the boat.

Lily stared at the men as they helped. "Run. Hurry." She grabbed one of the little boys, who ran by himself and tripped and fell. Picking him up as he began to cry, she held him close to her and ran to the fishing vessel. When she heard the pounding of the soldier's boots, fear knotted inside her as she saw the nun hold up her hand to silence them.

"Shush, shush." The nun put her index finger to her lips.

Lily's mind froze. She felt as if a hand closed around her throat and her breath solidified.

"Get behind the crates," whispered the nun. "The soldiers are changing their routine. We never counted on this. Hopefully, they won't find us." The fishermen and nun hugged the children to them. They ducked behind the crates. "Good, they didn't stop and have started to the dock office. As soon as they get a safe distance away from us, we'll get on the boat."

Lily kept the child she held close to her chest. Her body stiffened in shock and she grit her teeth. Her heart jumped in her chest as he whimpered. "Shush. shush," she whispered in his ear and held the little boy tighter, hoping the pounding of the soldier's boots would hide his whimpering. Blood began to pound in her temples as she hid.

When the soldiers moved out of sight, Lily swallowed hard, squared her shoulders, and ran. She rushed to the deck of the boat and stared as the fishermen with the children scurried onto the deck of the fishing boat. "Get under the nets," she whispered to each one as they passed her. After all the children were on the boat's deck, she looked back. The nun stood beside the vessel. Startled, she stood very still and listened. A voice called out to the nun.

"Come on, Sister." A thin man in a ragged, dirty white shirt with blue-gray stripes hung from his shoulders and looked about three sizes too big. His eyes were sunk deep in his head. He ran toward the nun. When he reached her, he stood at her side. He seemed to be pleading with the nun. Finally, Lily saw the sister shrug and motioned to him to follow her.

"I don't know. Oh...All right." *Can we take one more?* The nun mouthed from the dock to the captain as he stood at the wheel watching the children crawl under the nets.

"He can come aboard. But no more. He can hide in the cupboard here." The captain pointed in front of him. "No more passengers."

"Thank you, Captain." The nun smiled.

"What's going on?" Lily asked as the nun stepped on the deck of the boat. The man followed with a slight limp. He coughed as he pushed past Lily. His shoes, clogs of the Dutch type, clomped as he walked. Bending down in front of the wheel cabin, he crawled into the cupboard and curled up.

"He told me he escaped from a prisoner camp and had to get out of Poland. He didn't want to get caught and executed," the nun said.

"He looks as if he is sick. He's coughing and shaking." Lily watched the passenger.

"He might be. The prisoners are starved even though they are forced to work at hard labor. Many of them are sick. We'll try to keep him away from the children."

The nun looked at the fishermen as they began to load the empty barrels on the back of the deck. "Lily, make sure all the children are under the nets. Put the little child you are carrying near to where you will be."

Lily laid the little boy down and covered him with a net. "I'll be right back."

"And here, Lily, please give the man in the cupboard this handkerchief to cover his mouth." She handed Lily a handkerchief from the pocket of her habit. "Hurry, the soldiers are looking our way. I don't think they can see us, but maybe they'll come back if they think something is wrong because the boat is not moving out to sea fast enough." When the last barrel was hoisted onto the deck.

"The soldiers look as if they might come back and check on us. Get the motor going," the captain said.

Lily covered the man with a blanket the captain handed to her.

The fishermen started to sing a boat song as the captain started the boat's motor and moved out to sea. He steered the boat toward Sweden.

"Children, be very quiet," the sister whispered when the children begin to talk to each other.

"We're not far enough out to sea yet," Lily murmured. Propped up on her elbow, she peeked through the net, and stared at the dock. There were three soldiers who had walked on the dock and stood near the slip where the fishing boat had just been docked. They waved to the captain as they smoked their cigarettes.

With her head low, she sat up. Leaning back on the side of the boat, she bent her knees, hugging them to her. The white sand of the dunes, lights of the small towns, and docks along the coast dim as the boat drove through the waves of the Baltic Sea. The gray sky began to disappear as the sun rose. When the boat was far enough out to sea and she was unable to see the shoreline, Lily stood. "All right, children." She sighed. *I better count before we get to far out to sea.* She pulled back the nets and counted. "One, two…We have ten. Thank goodness. Why didn't I do this before we left?"

"No. Quick. Pull the nets over them. I hear the motor of a boat." The captain pointed to a boat bouncing up and down as it sped toward the fishing boat. "There it is."

Lily peeked over the side and in the direction the captain pointed.

"What is it?" Lily asked.

"It's a German patrol boat. Hurry everyone get back under the nets. You and the nun too." The captain yelled over the noise of his motor and the motor of the boat nearing them.

Lily kept down as she helped the nuns throw the nets over the children and then helped pushed the nun and herself under the nets next to them. Icy fear twisted around Lily's heart. Her stomach was clenched tight. Her body stiffened. Lily hugged her arms around her as she lay very still under the net.

Lily heard the German soldier yell to the captain as he pulled close to the fishing boat. His motor slowed down. "It's you in the front today. We're watching. You were slow moving out to sea, but the other boats were slower."

She could hear the patrol boat bumping against the fishing boat as it moved up and down slapping against the waves as she waited for it to motor back to the docks. Remaining motionless, she shivered with panic. She could sense the color drained from her face as she touched her cold cheek. Her stomach clenched tight. Her pulse began to beat erratically as the German spoke.

"What do you want?" The captain slowed and idled his motor.

"Get out to sea. The other ships are following and catching up. We'll try to slow them up while you find a good spot. We want you to get a good place to throw your nets. Our soldiers need food. We'll be waiting for you to get back. You always bring back a good catch."

"Thanks." The captain waved as the patrol boat turned and sped to the fishing boats following behind them. "The

Germans haven't discovered what we do yet. But one of these days we may run into a smart one, who will figure it out. Hopefully not soon." The captain laughed as he yelled to the nun and Lily when they crawled out from the nets. "We hope to confuse the Germans by not using the same boat to carry escaping people from Poland. The boat carrying passengers is always the first one to leave the docks, so we mix up who goes first. If the soldiers search any of the ships it's usually the last one."

"Okay, children, you can come out," Lily called to them. "Be careful, the sea is rough and the boat is really rolling from side to side. Stay in the middle of the deck." She watched as they tried to walk, finally sitting on the nets and talking to each other.

Lily looked intently at the nun. "I heard the man in the cupboard cough once or twice while the Germans were beside our boat. I didn't hear him cough again. I'm worried. Do you think he's all right?"

She walked toward the wheel off the ship, rubbing off the spray of the waves as it hit her cheeks. "The ship is rocking so hard it's difficult to walk." Holding onto anything she could grab made it easier for her walk to the captain's wheel.

Bending down, she opened the cupboard door and stared at the man's pale face. The handkerchief was stuffed in his mouth. "Are you all right?" Lily watched him. He didn't move. Quickly, she pulled the handkerchief from his mouth and waited for him to take a breath. With her hand held in front of his mouth, she tried to feel a breath but didn't feel any. His chest was not moving. She waited a few minutes. Pushing him on his side, his back toward her, she slapped his back hard. "Thank God." His chest move a little. She hit him again. He coughed and took a deep breath "He's breathing, but he's shaking. Do you have another blanket, Captain?"

"Look over there." The captain pointed to the drawer on the other side of the cupboard.

Lily wiggled the drawer. "It seems to be stuck."

"The salt water doesn't help. Things don't seem to work the way they are supposed to. Pull on it as hard as you can."

"Finally." Lily sighed as she yanked a blanket off the pile and covered the man. "You'll be warmer now." Tucking the blanket around him, she watched him attempt to smile as he closed his eyes. She left the door open and strolled around the deck, checking on the children, making sure they were all right and warm. "If you feel cold, let me know. I'll give you another blanket," she said to each one.

Lily sat down, leaned against the side of the boat, and stared out to sea. It was calming down. The boat tilted side to side and the back and forth motion lulled her to sleep.

The captain's voice woke her. "We'll be in neutral waters in a few minutes. Get all the children up. We have to be fast when we transfer them."

Lily rubbed her eyes as she stood up. "Children, we're almost ready to start the transfer onto the other ship."

"As soon as we see the ship with the large light blue and yellow flags painted on its sides get near to us be ready. It's the ship that will take you to Sweden." She pointed to the ship in the distance. "See it. It will be here very soon." We have to get ready to board it. Wrap your blankets around you."

"We will pull up close to the ship and move the children and man by dingy to it. We'll have to hurry." The captain waved to the men on the Swedish ship. "The Swedish ships resting in the harbor send out coded messages to all the ships when they see German patrol boats spying on us," the captain said. "Often the Germans watch Denmark and Sweden with patrol boats the ships in dock can't see. I don't see any now, but they appear out of nowhere sometimes."

"The Swedes are neutral. We're in their waters now," Lily said. "We should be safe."

"Yes. But if the Germans figure out what we fisherman are doing, they will capture our boats before we reach Swedish waters and safety. They'll seize us and put us to death," the captain answered.

She raised her hand and waved. "They're lowering their small boats into the water."

"I see the Swedish ship and there aren't any patrol boats around." The nun stared into the sea.

"Good." The captain turned the wheel of his ship and motored toward the Swedish ship "Get the children in a line. We are near enough for the transfer. The Swedes are putting two boats in the water. Five children in a boat. The man will go in the second boat."

Lily made sure the children were all awake. "Come on, children. It's time to change boats and go to Sweden where you will be free and safe." Gently leading them to the side of the boat where a rope ladder hung, she waited. "Let's all hold hands." She smiled as she watched two sailors climb from their ship and into their dinghies. They rowed toward the fishing boat. The first sailor to reach the Danish boat climbed the rope ladder to the first step and reached over the side of the boat to pick up a child.

"This man will help you go down the ladder to a smaller vessel and help you into the big ship." She hugged the Swedish sailor who stood at her side.

"My name is Bjorn."

"See where you are going. It's the ship with the blue and yellow paint." Her finger pointed to the ship. "Bjorn will help you," Lily said to each child.

"Please, Bjorn, wait right here. There's one more passenger." She moved to the wheel, leaned down in front of the open cabin, and shook the sleeping man. With difficulty, he rose on shaky legs and rubbed his eyes.

"Come on. It's time to go. Stand with the children. Wrap your blanket around you. You're shaking."

Lily watched one of the fishermen hold on to the side of the boat and help the children to the first step of the ladder. He handed the small children into Bjorn's arms who carried each one down to the dingy then returned for the next one. When it was the older children's turn, Bjorn held onto them as he walked ahead of them to the small boat. Lily gave each child a hug as they went over the side of the boat. "Enjoy your new home," she whispered to each child as they left. The second sailor repeated the same procedure. She was surprised when one of the eldest girls handed her a cardboard covered book before she turned and climbed over the side to the first step of the ladder.

"It's what I wrote about when I was in the Ghetto and about how the nuns helped me escape from the Germans. The girl hugged Lily. "Please see that it gets to the nuns at the convent. The nuns will hide it. People must see what life was like after the Germans came to Poland."

"I will be very careful with it and see that Mother Superior gets it. There's a family waiting for you. You will have a very good life from now on."

The man, who begged the nun to take him stood beside her. "Goodbye. You are safe now." She smiled. "Bjorn, this man needs a doctor. He's ill," she said to the sailor as he began to help him down the ladder.

"Good luck," she called to the children, staring at the sea, as each sailor began to row their dingy to the Swedish ship.

"Why is that boat motoring toward us, Sister?" Lily wrapped her arms around herself.

"They are bringing us root vegetables and cabbage. We bring food to the people in the Ghetto and some of the small villages we passed through on our way here. We leave fish also."

Lily sat back and sighed. *It's finished. The children are safe.* The deep furrows in her forehead began to relax. The Swedish ship disappeared over the horizon as she watched.

As the fishermen turned and motored back to the docks in Poland, they started throwing their nets into the sea. Dragging them through the water, the wriggling fish were hauled in. They dumped their catch into the bin in the middle of the boat. After the bin was filled, they unloaded them into the barrels the nuns owned. *We'll go back to Gdansk with a full vessel of fish.*

Standing and walking around the fishermen as they worked, she finally sat and leaned against the wheel house wall, opened the book the girl gave her and began to read in the bright daylight.

She flipped through the diary. *It looks as if she wrote an entry every day. The dates cover three weeks.*

Turning back to the first page's label, she read.

"The first thoughts."

We are struggling with starvation. People are dying. The nuns help us, but there are so many who need assistance.

As Lily read on she realized the girl criticized herself bitterly when she lost her willpower and ate her meager rations all at once when it was handed to her instead of saving some of her food for later. Tears covered her cheeks as she read on.

"A week later."

I can't believe I will ever be allowed to leave this horrible place without a yellow six point star pinned to my dress. I don't believe God exists. I see people shot by soldiers because they don't move fast enough, even though they are old and sick.

"Five days later."

I have a feeling I'm writing for the last time, but I sense there is something in the air. A nun has found a way to smuggle me out of my prison and hide me in the convent.

"Two days later"

I'm learning very hard to recite the prayers and catechism of the sisters, so the Germans will not know I'm Jewish. The nuns will take us to Sweden. I will live. I may never see my family and friends again, but I will live.

"What are you doing, Lily?" the nun called.

"I'm reading the diary one of the children gave me."

"We have collected many of them. We hide them under the floor boards. Someday the world will know what happened here."

Lily wiped the tears from her cheeks with the back of her hand and closed the diary. "Will it take us as long to get home as it did to get to the docks?"

"It will be an easy trip back to the convent. We can travel during the daylight since the children are gone. The Germans are usually gathering up prisoners or fighting Partisans so they don't bother with us. If we meet them, they take some food like I told you, but they don't usually have room in their jeeps for much. We promise to bring them some food when we get back to the convent. We never do. If they come to the convent and demand that we make good on our promise, we say we forgot and will make good on our next trip." The nun joined Lily behind the wheel house.

"The boat is just about ready to dock. Hide under the nets while the fishermen unload the barrels and load them into the wagon," the captain said. "When they finish unloading the barrels, the soldiers should be at the gate. Run to the cart and get going. We don't want them to start questioning you."

"But if they are at the dock when we pull in pretend you're helping. It's dark so they will not know where you came from. Don't worry, they are lazy and don't ask many questions. I think they are afraid we'll ask them to help us unload. If they think you went out on the boat, it doesn't matter. They don't care." The captain smiled.

The fishermen loaded the wagon with no interference from the Germans.

Lily held her breath until the nun waved to the Germans as she drove through the dock entrance.

We're on our way to the convent. Lily hummed to herself and watched the scenery. *Poland is really beautiful.*

As the nun headed east out of town, she whipped the horses. She leaned to Lily. "Lily, Lily."

"What? What is it? I'm sorry I didn't hear your question."

"Do you know how to ski?"

"Yes. Why do you ask?"

"We'll be going over the Tatra Mountains at the end of the week and need a group of Partisans to go with us. We take families on these trips."

"How do you smuggle them out?"

"We have them hidden in the salt mines in Krakow. It's a good place to leave from. The Germans are in the mines. They act the way they do in the forest. They don't want to go very deep so they don't get trapped and killed. They stay close to the surface while they manufacture their munitions, but we go deep into the mine. There is an entrance in the back. The Germans haven't found it yet."

"It's dangerous for these Partisans isn't it?"

"Yes. They have to be very careful. But they are able to commit some espionage while they wait. No one knows they're there. The workers are prisoners. They don't tell if they see them. They help distract the soldiers when we leave. Want to go with us? We could use your help."

"I'll go with you. Maybe I can get Rachel to come with us. How long a trip is it?"

"I hope she will. We need all the help we can get. The trip takes about two weeks. We take the families into Slovakia. Another group picks them up and takes them through Austria and then to Switzerland, another neutral country."

I need to get back to my time, first. Lily watched a thick fog roll over the landscape as they neared the convent. As it got thicker, she jumped from her seat when the nun stopped the wagon near the chapel of the convent.

CHAPTER TEN

October 10, 2014

It was hard for Lily to focus her eyes, they strained to see what surrounded her. The sounds she heard were different from the ones around the convent. The sound of moving water, of car horns, and cars on the road awoke her. When the fog cleared, she found herself standing in the garden of Rachel's home. A figure stood at the river bank. It was Rachel's housekeeper, Anna.

"Anna," she called. "What are you doing?"

"Just taking a little break. The water is so restful."

"Is Rachel here?"

"No. I think she went to Krakow. There was an errand she had to do."

"Is Karl around?"

"He was here last night, but he had to go to France this morning. Rachel took her car. The plan was for her to take him to the airport, then drive into Krakow.

Maybe Rachel knew the nuns were going on a trip over the Tatra Mountain Range and went there to see if she could join them. I want to go also. She had to find her friend. "Can I get to Krakow by bus?"

"Yes. The bus depot is in the village square. The office where you buy your ticket is in the back behind the wishing well."

"What time do the buses leave?"

"Nine, noon, and four. The roads are mostly four lanes so, the buses can go eighty miles an hour. It only takes about three to four hours to get there."

Lily pushed up the sleeve of her sweater and glanced at her watch. "I have time to write a column about the Champagne Reception and make the noon bus if I hurry. I'll get there at a good time." She turned and ran to the door near the patio. Shoving it open, she ran down the hall, and up the stairs to her room.

Lily dragged out her computer and typed as fast as she could. Rereading it, she thought what a good description she wrote about where, what, and why the reception was held and the description of the food would make the readers see how sophisticated the event was. She added a few paragraphs about the music. Glancing at her watch she quickly e-mailed it to her boss. *Well, now I've sent two articles. I better think up a good excuse about why there have only been two messages. The tape of Anika's show will help.*

Lily ran to the bathroom. After a quick shower, she dressed in jeans and a turtleneck sweater. *If I'm going up the mountains there will be snow. I'll need my waterproof boots and a heavy jacket.* She pushed back her clothes and pulled her waterproof boots from the back of the armoire. *I didn't bring a warm jacket. I'll look in Rachel's room.* Fixing her makeup, she pulled some Zloty, the local currency, and her passport from her purse. Sticking them in her jean pocket, she ran to the master bedroom and hunted through Rachel's closet. *Here's one.* She pulled a hooded parker from a hanger and ran to the kitchen.

Anna stood at the stove. When she heard Lily's footsteps, she stopped stirring the soup she had just made.

Lily stopped for a moment. If she was able to meet up with her friend, they would go to the salt mine before the trip to the mountains. The nun who went to the dock with me let on that's where the people smuggled out over the mountain were left before they started on their trip. It would be dark in the mine. "Do you have a flashlight?"

"There's one in the drawer by the refrigerator. It's under the papers," Anna said, as she stirred the soup in the pot on the stove. "Do you want something to eat before you go?"

"No thanks. I'll miss the bus if I take the time to eat." Lily glanced at the newspaper as she pushed it out of the way to open the drawer. The headlines screamed out at her. *Works of World War II Polish and Jewish survivors honored at the new museum in Krakow.* She grabbed the flashlight and stuffed it in her back pocket. "See you later." Lily threw the words over her shoulder as she pushed open the side door. Waving, she smiled at Anna.

She jogged to the wall and turned left on the main street, holding the jacket under her arm. The sweets in the bakery window cried out to her as she passed. Glancing at her watch, she backed up, ran up the stairs, and threw open the door of the bakery. "May I have a doughnut, Elka?"

"Sure. Where's Rachel?" she said as she folded a paper napkin around the doughnut.

"Rachel is in Krakow. I'm going to meet her there. I'd better go, I need to take the bus. It should be here in a few minutes." Lily stuck her free hand in her pocket.

"No. It's my treat."

"Thanks." She ran to the depot, knocked on the closed door of the ticket office, and waited for the Station Master to open it. She took a large bit of her sweet and chewed.

"You just made it, young lady. The bus is just coming up the street and will be pulling into the square if that's the one you're taking."

"Krakow?"

"Yes, that's the one you want."

Her hand dug into her pocket of her jeans and pulled out some Zloty to pay for her ticket. "Do you happen to have a map of Krakow?"

The agent handed her a ticket and map just as the bus pulled in and stopped.

"Do you have luggage?" the driver asked when she handed him her ticket.

"No." She stared up the aisle as she climbed the last step. The bus was packed. There were only two seats open. Lily selected the one behind the driver.

Opening the map she studied the city of Krakow. *Where would Rachel go while she waited for the nuns? I know. To the museum.* She watched the villages and farmland as the bus flew to the main square of Krakow. The memory of the burned out houses and buildings and the bombed earth of WWII made her shudder. What she had seen in the 1940s had recovered and was beautiful.

As Lily ran down the stairs of the bus, she looked around the square. Her friend's car was parked near the municipal buildings. She peered up at the pole and street sign beside her. "Okay, I'm on Parvia Street that's the one I want." She examined the map. "Walk straight, then turn left on Rowsina, right on Dajwov." *I'm, here in Kazimiers, the Jewish quarters.* She looked around.

"Rachel," she called and waved to her friend. "I knew you'd be here," she said as her friend ran down the steps of the Galicia Museum.

"I thought I'd wait and see if I could get back to the nun's time. If we can get back to there and meet up with them, we can help them go over the Tatra Mountains," Rachel stated.

"I want to go too. The nun told me about the trip on the way back from the Baltic Sea. I think we're in luck. It's supposed to get foggy and rainy later today."

"If the nuns are here and we go back to the war, we'll find them," Rachel said.

"I borrowed your jacket."

"That's fine. Wait while I get the one I wore. I left it in the museum."

"It's starting to rain and it's getting foggy and misty. We need to go to the Wieliczk Salt Mines." Rachel threw her jacket over her shoulders.

The nun also told me there is a secret entrance. It's in the back. I'm sure it's closed up now, but during the war it was there." She glanced at her watch. "We're running out of time."

"I hope we find the back door leading us to the lower floors because the fog is lifting and it's beginning to look like we're back in the 1940s."

March 1943

"Follow me, Lily. I know a short-cut to the mines. We'll go to the front and wait. There's an elevator now that takes you to the lower levels. I don't think it ran during World War II. If we get to the mine before we get back to the 1940s, we can take it. Today there is only one way in and the same way out."

"Be careful." Rachel pulled Lily into the bushes at the front of the building. "A truckload of soldiers is coming down the street. We're in the 1940s. Too late, we'll have to get to the back of the building."

"Okay. As soon as they pass we'll go around back and search for the entrance."

"Are they stopping?"

"No. They must be on their way to one of the camps in Krakow. Mother Superior said they keep a small staff of soldiers at the mine. Prisoners do all the work."

"Do the soldiers go deep into the mine?"

"It's about a thousand feet deep. Mother Superior said the Germans stay in the second or third level to make their missiles, bombs, and other ammunitions. It's like the woods. They don't want to get caught too far underground. They want to be where they can escape quickly in case of sabotage. Also sometimes, if there are heavy rains, the lower levels flood."

"The truck is gone. If we hurry we can get to the back of the mine before anyone else comes." Rachel motioned to Lily. "Follow me." She turned the corner and ran.

"What happens if any of the prisoners see us?"

"The nuns told me they don't tell. The Partisans usually cut the phone lines. So the soldiers can't call in guards if they need help or in case there's an uprising. Also, the prisoners are transported from labor camps and are forced to work in this underground armament factory. They hate the soldiers. The prisoners cause trouble or start a fight to distract the guards if they see the nuns. This is when the nuns and families escape. Sometimes even one of the prisoners tries to escape with the nuns."

"I guess if one or two leave no one figures out when they escaped. The soldiers only find out the prisoners are missing when they get back to camp. They don't do a count until then."

When they reached the back of the mine, Lily looked around. The moon was full and shined on the building. "I see the nun's wagon. It's close to the building, behind the stack of crates over there." Her finger pointed to the pile of boxes. "The nuns must be in the mine with the families waiting for the right time to leave."

Lily stared at the back wall. "Come here, Rachel. It looks as if this piece of wood doesn't quite meet the wall.

See the section of the planks in front of me." Bending down, she ran her hand over the boards, stopping at the bottom of the slats. "A button. This must be the secret door." She stabbed it with her index finger.

The crunching and squeaking of the wall as it scraped along the ground made Lily uneasy. "I hope the soldiers don't hear the noise. Put your jacket on it'll be easier than carrying them," Lily said as she slipped hers on.

"Hear the loud pounding and rumbling of their machinery? It's a wonder they can ever hear again after being down there listening to the noise all day." Rachel laughed softly.

Lily pulled her quickly through the door as it started to close.

"It's a good thing I took a flashlight from your house. It's so dark. I can't see anything." Lily pushed on the light. "It looks as if we're in a long hallway." Her shoulder rubbed against the wall. "It's cold."

"It's salt." Rachel said. "Shine the light on it. See. Its various shades of gray make it look like granite. After many processes, it becomes the white salt we have at the table or use in cooking."

"We're going down. It's getting colder. I hope we find the nuns soon." Lily shined the flashlight on the floor as they walked deeper into the mine. *I wanted to make sure if we pass a room where the Germans are working they wouldn't see the light moving on the walls.*

"It feels as if we're going on a journey to the center of the Earth," Rachel said.

"Stop. I hear voices, Lily."

Lily stopped and listened. She grabbed Rachel's hand and started down a staircase to another long hallway. "I think the voices are coming from below us. Let's keep walking and see if it's the nuns." As she walked the voices got louder. The hallway led to another staircase. She walked down the steps and was stopped suddenly by a wall. "The only way we can go is back," Lily said.

There was a doorway on her left and one on her right. Lily paused on the last step. Feeling Rachel lurch into her, she grabbed onto the left-hand door jamb to prevent from stumbling to the floor. "Sorry I didn't mean to stop so suddenly."

"Ouch," Rachel whimpered.

"What's wrong?"

"I stubbed my toe when I bumped into you."

"Shush. Shush." With her index finger to her lips, she whispered, "The voices are coming from inside the room to my left," she pointed to her left and whispered as she peeked around the corner of the doorway.

"It's all right. It's Mother Superior with some people." She dragged Rachel into a large empty room. Blankets laid around the floor.

"Hello, girls." Mother Superior stared at them. "We were just about ready to go. I'm glad you got here before we had to leave. We need your help."

"Hello, Mother." Lily ran to the nun and hugged her. "My trip to the Swedish waters was successful. We're ready to help here."

"All right people, fold up the blankets. Let's return to the back entrance and our transportation, the wagon. More blankets and warm clothes are there. Lily, climb with me to the outside since you have a flashlight. Rachel, you walk at the rear of the group. Make sure everyone keeps up."

When the nun reached the secret door, she pushed on the waist-high button next to the door on her right. As the door slid open she peeked out. "We're in the open there's no shelter, but it's clear. So run. We don't want to get caught."

Lily watched the nun count her passengers as she helped them into the wagon. "Some of the families look very frail," she said slipping the flashlight into her pocket. "Will they make the trip?"

"They are pretty frail but they have the will to get to a place where they are safe. I haven't lost anybody yet. We'll walk the wagon and horses until we get a good distance away to run them. We don't want the Nazis to hear the pounding of their hooves. We need to be in the mountains by the time it gets light out."

The Partisans will go with the families in the wagon and hide them under the hay. We'll ride up front.

"How many people?" Lily asked.

"There are four families, eight parents and six children, one man who slipped away from his work detail, two Partisans and the three of us. Twenty in all. We need more help because it's harder to get over the mountains. We each have to carry a bag with supplies, except for the little children. If there's snow it's worse and there will be snow at this time of the year."

When it was time to run the horses, the nun jumped up to the seat and extended her hand helping Lily and Rachel get onto the wagon seat. "We're going up the mountain and over to the Slovakia side. The horses and wagon will only go so far. The slopes get too steep for them to pull a wagon. But we'll be able to ride for a while. We have to walk or ski the last part of the trip. We carry some skis under the wagon and borrow others along with sleds from the villagers. The Partisans will guide us. There will be lots of snow. Sometimes it covers lakes so we have to be very careful. We'll also have to help the parents with their children.

"There will be chair lifts to help on the upper part of the trip and a gondola lift to assist us over the Goryczkwia Valley and to the Slovakia side of the mountain. The Gerlach Peak is 871 feet high. This is where we go over the valley. It will be bitter cold up there. We will need the warm clothes I brought in the bags we're carrying."

"Where are the Partisans going?" Lily watched the men traveling with them jump from the wagon.

"They're going into the small town, just around the boulder and the thick trees ahead, to meet the villagers who help us. And check to see if there are any enemies lurking about. We'll wait here for them to come back."

"Do we have food?" Lily asked.

"Some of the mountain people have cheese, bread, and milk for the children, sausages and dried fruit. They give it to us. They raise sheep and usually have woolen things for our passengers. Many resistance workers live in the mountains. In-between sabotaging German locations, they raise animals, weave, and make clothes."

Lily shivered. "It's getting colder." She watched the Partisans come back carrying burlap bags over their shoulders and dragging skis.

"Good, they brought some food and the extra skis." The nun reached behind her and pulled a blanket from the pile next to one of the children. "Put this around yourself." The nun passed the blanket to Lily. "Our first stop will be Bilekova Chata. It's a hut. Skiers stay there sometimes. That's the one place the soldiers don't check. It's not comfortable for them. Wooden bunks and no place to cook. We're going to stay there for the night. After that, we have to walk. We have to look after the children. Even though their parents have more energy, they aren't very healthy. It takes all their energy to climb. I'll hide the wagon in the woods next to the village. We'll walk or ski from now on."

"Do the Germans patrol the mountains?" Lily asked.

"Yes. Somehow they have figured out the mountains are a hiding place for the Partisans so they check the villages at odd hours to make sure the owners of the homes are where they are supposed to be, at home or work."

Lily started to help the men and women brush the hay from their clothes as they crawled from the wagon. *Mother*

Superior is right. The passengers seemed to have developed energy they didn't have at the beginning of the trip. She passed out the cross-country skis hidden under the wagon. The last things she pulled from the wagon were two large sleds.

"Who are these for?" Lily asked.

"The people who are not strong enough to ski will be pulled by the Partisans. You girls carry the children."

"That's all right Mother Superior. We can do that," one of the Partisan said.

"We're going to try to stay on the paths in the pine trees as we climb. The Partisans will stay on the edge." The snow crunched under her skis.

I'm glad I wore my boots. I can hold the skis on better. After helping a child onto the huge granite boulder on the path and watching him crawl to the top, Lily looked around and then at the little boy. "Come on." Her arms and hands moved in front of her. She bent fingers toward her indicating he slide down the other side and into her arms.

"Are you cold?" She wrapped her arms around herself and pretended to shiver. Watching the boy nod yes, she pulled open the zipper of her bag to remove a scarf, and wrapped it around his neck, chin, and nose then stuffed the ends into his jacket. Lastly, she pulled his cap over his ears and down to his eyebrows. Grabbing his mitten-covered hand, she set his feet on top of hers with his body facing her so he could hang onto her knees and let her poles do most of the work as she trudged through the snow. *My muscles are really working. Thank goodness I did all that training in London.*

They skied for a long time before the nuns let them stop. Sitting in the snow, she removed food from a sack and handed it out.

"We're almost at the hut." The nun smiled.

"The children are very tired." Lily slipped off her skis and put them and the poles on one of the sleds. She picked up the little boy she was with and carried him as she trudged through the snow. "There it is. I see the hut," she whispered in the boy's ear. "See?" She pointed in front of her.

Lily looked at Rachel. "You look very tired."

"I am. Not use to so much exercise."

You're tired. You skied alone, I had a passenger. She smiled at her friend.

"Come on, let's get a bunk," Lily said to Rachel as she stomped snow off her boots before she entered the hut and watched her friend select the bed next to the door as she took one near a window.

Soon everyone was settled on a bunk. The nun handed out more food and cups filled with snow. "We need water, as the snow melts we get it. It's starting to get dark."

Lily sat on her bunk and stared out the window. The stars and moon on a black sky shined into the glassless window. It was a clear night. The crisp cold air blew across her bunk. Wrapping a blanket around her, she leaned out the window. *Maybe if I could stand on something high I could reach a star.*

Lily awoke to the sun coming over the mountain. Its rays caught the snow, making it sparkle. "Is that coffee you're holding, Mother Superior? Thank goodness. I need a cup. I thought we couldn't cook."

"We can't. It's cold but strong.

"We melted some snow and added ground coffee. It won't be like you're used to, but it will wake you up as you get some caffeine." The nun handed Lily a cup and watched her face as she took a sip. "That bad?" She laughed.

"It's terrible, but it woke me up," Lily said, as she took a couple of sips.

"Are you ready?" one of the Partisans asked. "We better move in case the soldiers come by. We have a report they were in the village we stopped at yesterday."

"I need some coffee," Rachel said.

"Here, finish mine." Lily handed her the cup. She laughed when she saw Rachel also wrinkle her nose after she took a sip.

"Clean everything up. If the soldiers decide to look in this hut, we don't want them to know anyone has been here." Mother Superior picked up her bag and looked around the building before she moved out of the hut.

As Lily's boots crunched in the snow, she touched her face. "It's beginning to snow. My cheeks are wet." Pulling a scarf around her face, she kept only her eyes uncovered. All of a sudden, gales of snow whirls surrounded her. It didn't let up as she stumbled when her boots slipped on an icy rock and her feet flew out from under her as she landed in a pile of snow. Lily watched the nun run to her through the snow. The rocks were treacherous to walk on, but it was better than skiing.

"Are you all right? It will be easier in a few minutes. We'll be at a chair lift. The lift goes to Zakopane. We'll be safe there. The Partisans say the Germans haven't been in that area for quite a while."

Lily sighed when she reached the lift. *A rest. Finally.* "The snow has let up."

"Snowstorms come up without warning and leave just as fast," the nun said.

When everyone was settled in a chair, the nun pulled the lever starting the lift. "We're going into a valley."

The snow eased as she reached the bottom of the lift. She stared at the chalets close to the building where the motor of the lift was housed. The houses were painted in bright colors, skis and poles were stuck in the snow next to their front doors and snow was pushed up against the lodges. Smoke billowed from their chimneys. When the nun shut off the chair lift, she stomped through the snow to a house ahead of her. Lily grabbed Rachel and followed.

"I smell real coffee this time." Lily laughed. "Which house are we going to?"

"To the one where the woman is standing in the doorway and waving to us," Rachel said watching the nun wave back to the woman.

Lily knocked the snow off her boots on the side of the house before she entered the chalet. A table was set with coffee, sweet rolls, and meats in the room inside the door. Hunger overtook her. She didn't think she could wait until everyone sat down to take a sweet roll, but she did.

A fire blazed in the large fireplace. Lily motioned for Rachel to come to her.

They strolled to the mantel, stretched their arms over the hearth, and stood there letting the warmth fill their bodies.

Finally, everyone arrived and sat at the table. Lily moved to the sideboard and poured herself a cup of coffee. Walking back to the fire, she sipped it while she thought about the next part of their journey.

"Mother Superior told me we're going to get some sleep and then use our skis to climb to another chair lift and then a gondola lift. Then we'll get to the Slovakia side of the mountain range," Rachel said as she joined her.

How are these poor people going to ski down the mountain? Oh well, I'm sure Mother Superior has a plan. It's probably the sleds we used before. Right now I want to get some sleep. Lily went to the table and picked up a sweet roll, sat in an empty seat, and finished it. "Where's our hostess?"

"She's in the barn working," Rachel answered.

Lily was just about to pour herself another cup of coffee when she heard the pounding of boots.

"The Germans are on their way into town. Hide your dishes in the closet and food in the ice box."

"Hurry. We have to get out of here. I need to pack up my things. Come on, Rachel. Grab your stuff," Lily called to her friend.

Rachel followed Lily as she ran from the house. She could hear the rumble of tanks and trucks as she ran to the chair lift.

Lily shivered with panic. Slipping on her cross country skis, she skied through the trees using muscles she didn't even know she had. Her stomach clenched tight. A soft gasp escaped her then she panted with terror as she skied. *Where is the little boy I was with yesterday?* She looked around. *Oh. Thank goodness, he's in one of the sleds being pulled by a Partisan.*

"Jump on the lift, Lily." Rachel stuck out her arm. Reaching forward, she grabbed Lily's arm helping Lily jump onto the seat in front of her.

Lily let her skis hang as the lift moved. The Partisans pulled the people who were on the sleds through the trees. When she looked back, she could see the villagers running behind them, brushing brooms over the snow to hide the ski tracks.

When the chair lift stopped, she heard the nun call to them. "Go straight ahead. You'll see a gondola lift. We will load up and go across the valley to the Slovakia side, landing on Wierch Peak."

Lily watched as the Partisans helped the families and loaded the sleds onto the gondola lift.

"It doesn't take everyone. I'll wait and go with you," Rachel cried out.

"Don't worry. As many of the families that can fit in will get on this gondola. The one over there comes back to this side as this one moves to the other side. When it lands, the rest of us will get on and get to your side. The Partisans will disable the one they are on as it goes into the terminal so it won't come back."

Lily watched the families with the Partisans leave the car. Quickly she pulled off her skis and leaped on the returning car with Rachel and the people who remained. Her fear started to calm down. However, her relief was short lived. Her breath seemed to cut off as the chair lift they'd just used started to move. A deep breath help her to relax.

"What's wrong, Lily?" Rachel asked.

Lily couldn't find her voice. With an anxious little cough, she pointed to the side of the valley they had both just left.

"I don't see anything."

"Pay attention. Look." Lily's pulse beat rapidly. "See it now?"

"Oh. The chair lift is moving."

"The Germans have seen our ski tracks. They are following. Even though we disabled the car and they can't get to the other side, they have rifles and they'll radio the German soldiers stationed on the Slovakia side. We should have stayed in the woods. Used those trails." The nun frowned at Lily and Rachel.

"Everybody duck down. The soldiers have reached the edge of the mountain. They are dressed all in white and are raising their guns." Lily's pulse beat erratically. With her clenched hands, her nails entered her palms when the soldiers began to shoot. She heard a whistling sound as a bullet flew by her head.

"It's fine. We'll make it." Lily sighed. "I don't think their bullets can reach us once we reach the terminal on the other side." There was a cry of relief from the occupants as the last gondola lift reached the Slovakia side.

"All right disable it. Everyone put on your skis, drag the sleds, and start down the mountain. See that group of pines?" The nun pointed to the trees halfway down the mountain. "Stop and go a few feet into the woods. There's a cave there. We'll hide in it. After we get to the trees take off your skis and brush away your footprints with pine branches as we walk through the woods," the nun said. "The Partisan will keep skiing and after a mile or two they'll stop, take off their skis and walk back pulling the sleds. They'll hide their tracks. Follow me."

Lily laughed. She saw the nun slip on skis and start down the mountain. Her habit blew in the breeze behind her so she looked like a bird. The group started down the Slovakia side.

When the group of families and Partisans gathered in the cave, Lily took out her flashlight, shinning it around the room they sat in. "This is perfect. We're protected from the snow." The warmth began to creep back into her body.

"We used to stay in the Castle of Kazmarok. It had nice beds, a place to cook, and we were warm, but the Germans took it over and our place is gone." The nun smiled at Lily. There is another town in Slovakia, Poprad. The resistance group from there helps us out. Groups from all over Poland and Slovakia have sprung up to help hide people the Germans want to exterminate."

The nun pulled one of the Partisans to the far end of the cave and whispered something to him. He gathered up his backpack and moved to the cave entrance.

"Everyone bundle up, we're going to be here for a while." The nun handed out blankets. A tense silence loomed over the group like a heavy mist. The families huddled together. "The Partisans will be contacting the group who will be taking you on to Austria and Switzerland. They will be telling them what has happened," the nun continued. "It will take a while for the other resistance workers to get here. They have to make sure it's safe."

"Here, take my watch. You'll need it to keep track of time."

Lily and Rachel followed the Partisan as he left the cave with his radio to signal the next group of resistance workers.

It started to snow again. A heavy mist floated across the mountain. Lily found it was hard to see the Slovakia villages at the foot of the Tatras. It was hard for her to hear Rachel calling her.

CHAPTER ELEVEN

October 10, 2014

"Rachel, I'm standing on blacktop. There's no snow. My jacket is wet so I was in the mountains. We are no longer outside the cave." Lily stared into the mist.

"No, Lily, you're right, we're in the parking lot outside the museum in Krakow." She looked up and saw the sun trying to break through the clouds as she walked toward her car in the square.

"What happened to the people and Mother Superior? Do you think they made it to a safe place?" A pain squeezed her heart as she thought about them. "Maybe we can go by the convent's cemetery and see if we can find a headstone for her."

"Come on. Get in the car. We'll drive to Warsaw and see if we can find out anything about what may have happened to her."

"I imagine it may be hard to find out any information. It's been over seventy years," Lily said as she followed her friend into her car.

Turning the key, Rachel started the motor and backed out of the space. "Your vacation is almost over. I wanted you to see the museum."

"Next time. I didn't get a cooking lesson either. But, I have the tape of her show. I can shop it around. I wrote an article about the Chopin Recital and Champagne Reception and sent it to my boss before I came to Krakow. So he won't be too mad I didn't do more."

"The car is slowing down and my foot is almost to the floor. And it's dark. What's going on? We're almost to Warsaw. We may have to walk a little to get help. The sky is filled with dark clouds. I hope it doesn't rain. Pull over to the side. Do you have your smartphone?"

"It's in the glove compartment."

April 10, 1943

"Never mind." As Lily leaned over to open it, she glanced out the window. She didn't bother to push the button of the glove compartment. "It's the nineteen-forties again." Lily looked intently at her surroundings. "Guess where we are?" Lily pointed to her left. "The Ghetto."

"Get out of the car and walk naturally. German soldiers are marching down the street. A truck is following them." Remembering the truck and soldiers at Rachel's house the day she arrived sent a cold chill up her back. It looks as if there is an officer in a jeep leading the group of soldiers. "Be careful. It's dark out. Maybe they won't see us."

Lily gasped, she realized a shiver of panic, and shuddered inwardly when they unexpectedly surrounded them. The general jumped out of the jeep.

"Papers. Papers," the officer yelled as he stood in front of them. The soldiers didn't wait for them to provide them. "Get into the truck." A soldier shoved them with the butt of his gun into the truck. After they reached the camp the same soldier herded them into a large room with no chairs. "Wait until you're called."

"Okay, Lily, what do we do now besides stand here and wait?"

"Shush, shush. Let me think…All right, when they start questioning us, follow me. Do what I do," she said as she sat on the floor watching the door open and close. The captured people were called in, then dragged out of the building. She looked around at the other people from the truck sitting with their heads down trying to hide the scared looks on their faces.

When the door to the other room swung open, Lily tried to see what was going on. She saw a woman hugging her little girl who was crying. Lily saw the officer who rode in the jeep. *Well it has to be our time now. There's no one else in the room.* The soldier nudged her and Rachel. *Finally.*

As she entered the office, Rachel stood behind her. The officer stood behind his desk leaning forward with the heels of his palms on the edge of the desk. He stared at them over the rim of his glasses. His uniform was black. He came out from behind his desk and paced back and forth with his hands behind his back. The leather soles of his shiny Jackboots pounded on the wooden floor.

At last, he spoke to them with cold sarcasm. His lips thinned as he spoke. "Why were you out after curfew?"

Lily lifted her chin and met his gaze head on. "We lost track of time." She bit her lip.

"We lost track of time is not an excuse. Tell me why you were out. I want an answer. Do we need to use a whip on you?"

Lily started to cough. Rachel copied her, coughing as hard as she could.

"Bite your lip," Lily whispered out of the side of her mouth.

"Are you sick?" His lips thinned with displeasure. "Answer me." His brows furrowed as he raised his hand and slapped her face.

Lily's winced. Her face throbbed from his slap.

"Do you have Tuberculosis? Answer me. You're coughing and bringing up blood. It's running down your chin," he screamed.

Lily stared at his face. It was like a stone mask.

He watched them for a few minutes. "Get them out of here. Take them to Auschwitz-Birkenau."

A warning voice whispered in Lily's head. *This could be worse. I wish I could tell them they are going to lose the war.* Her body stiffened.

"Move." The soldier pushed them out of the building and into the truck waiting at the entrance of the building. It was crowded. They managed to squeeze into the two empty seats on the bench. The children were on the floor.

Lily lurched forward when the truck stopped. She and Rachel jumped down from the bed of the truck and stood with the others who rode with them. The children hugged their parent's leg and cried. She scanned the area. There were two rows of barbed wire fences surrounding the camp and towers at intervals with soldiers manning machine guns and watching. They stood on the platform and waited. *What are we waiting for?* In a few minutes, a long train of cattle cars pulled up and stopped. Soldiers unlocked the doors and tugged them open. Men, women, and children poured out of the cars each carrying a suitcase. Soldiers looked them over and shoved them into lines on the platform in front of the cattle car.

Lily looked up as the driver of the truck pushed them into the group. The officers, sitting at tables next to doctors in white coats with stethoscopes hanging from their necks, yelled at the passengers. "Surrender all your belongings, papers, suitcases, and clothes." Virtually all their personal possession were left on the platform. "Take off your clothes," he yelled again. They were handed the striped clothes the prisoners were forced to wear. "Put these on your feet." He handed them clogs like the Dutch shoes. After they dressed they got in line again, the doctors signaled to them which line they should go to.

"This is not the time to play sick, Rachel. See those doctors, they're deciding who lives and who dies. Only the people who look well don't go to Block One. They stay alive. Even though their existence is very bad." Tears burned her eyes as the people who were not sent to Block One were tattooed with numbers on the inside of their left arm and marched to barracks. She wiped her eyes. When it was her and Rachel's turn, Lily saw a soldier whisper something in the doctor's ear whose line they were in. He didn't hesitate to send them away from Block One.

The soldier pulled them to the side and demanded they take off their clothes and put on a black and white striped dress over their underwear. She closed her eyes as she disrobed. *Why does he have to stare?*

He yelled as she began to kick her shoes to him. "Put these on." He handed her clogs and waited. They stood for several minutes.

Another soldier pulled Lily and Rachel from the group they stood with. "One of the officers has seen you and you will be given a special assignment. Just stay here."

They sat in the yard and waited.

Finally, the soldier returned. It was dark by the time they were assigned to a barracks. He led them to a long building with a cement floor. It had no windows. There were openings at either end without doors. There were very rudimental facilities running down the middle of the open room. Basic latrines and earthen-gutters over which forty-two taps had been installed. It was damp without electricity. There were holes in the roof. *No wonder it's damp. The rain comes in through the roof.* Lily saw rows of wooden bunk beds with straw mattresses. She counted sixty sleeping compartments in tiers of three beds. *One hundred and eighty people. It looks to me as if there are three or four women in each bed.* Lily climbed to the top bed. "Let's sleep together, Rachel. We have no blanket."

"Suppose we have sunny days. How are we going to escape?" Rachel asked.

The woman on the bed next to them leaned toward their bunk. "I took two blankets from the pile at the door. You can have one."

"Thank you." Lily smiled. "You are very sweet."

The woman began to whisper to them. "Some of the men escaped from the train we came in by removing the floor boards. Maybe we can do this if they transfer us to another camp by train. Some people escape from their work details. It's bad though. If the soldiers catch them, they kill not only the people who tried to escape, but ten more innocents."

"What do they do when they escape?"

"They get to the woods and hide. When they find a farmer's house, they watch the house for a while to see if the farmer and his family are loyal to the Partisans. If they see they are, they contact them.

You ladies look healthy. You could get jobs working at the generals' and other officers' homes. It would be easy to escape from there, especially if the guards watching you fall asleep."

"What's that smell?" Lily asked. Lily's eyes teared up. The thought of the men, women, and children she saw on the platform went through her mind.

"It's the smell from the crematorium."

"They say the soldiers tell the people they are going for a shower in Block One. Instead of water, they are gassed with a poison."

"I saw the bath sign on the door the doctors sent the people who looked sick. What do they do with the bodies?"

"They burn them or bury all of them in a big pit. That's what the few people who have escaped say. But they say it isn't done until they remove all their gold even their gold teeth."

Lily shuddered and lifted her hand to her cheek. It was ice cold.

She laid down and closed her eyes but didn't sleep. She watched the endless night gray into dawn through the open doorway.

"Wake up, Rachel. What job should we ask for?"

Before her friend could answer a woman soldier came to their bunks. "You two come with me, right now. The commandant wants to talk with you both. He'll let you into his office when he finishes his phone call."

They sat outside the office. "There's the woman who talked to us last night," Rachel said.

"What job do you have?" Lily asked.

Her face closed as if guarding a secret. "I sort through the prisoner's clothes. I can see that you get a warm jacket if you have something to trade."

"That's great. We'll see what we can trade. We'll have to find something," Lily said.

"Sit here and wait," the woman said as she pushed them into chairs sitting by the office door.

Finally, the office door opened.

"Come in," a woman who came out of the office said. "The commandant will see you now."

Lily entered the office with Rachel walking behind her, hanging on to her baggy dress. She stood in front of the desk waiting for him to acknowledge they were standing in front of him. When he turned, she paled. It was the officer who had questioned her the day she was put in the truck for the camp.

"Ladies, my wife needs help at the house. You are going to work and live there."

He doesn't recognize us. Thank God. Lily smiled. "I would be honored." She nudged Rachel.

"Me too. It's an honor."

"Go get in the truck outside the office. You'll be driven to my house."

"This is good, Rachel. Now we have a chance to escape," she whispered leaving the office.

Lily and Rachel cleaned and cooked. The officer's wife worked them as hard as she could while they waited for their time to escape.

Lily stood at the kitchen sink cleaning the breakfast dishes. "At least we have good food and a soft bed. Have you seen what the prisoners in the barracks get?" she asked Rachel as her friend selected china for the party tonight.

"Yes. Coffee for breakfast. Watery soup for lunch with meat four times a week and vegetables the other three days. They got three hundred to four hundred calories a day. For dinner, they ate nine hundred to one thousand calories consisting of bread, a small piece of sausage or small portions of jam and cheese."

"Oh no."

"What's wrong, Lily?"

"Look. They have hung three men. We have to get out of here."

That night after they served dinner at a party for officers and their mistresses or wives, their chance came. The officers let the guards have as much beer as they wanted. The guards who were supposed to be on guard were sound asleep.

Lily and Rachel tiptoed through the house. The women and men were all passed out in the living room where the musicians played. Lily stared at them. They were dressed in the clothes of the prisoner. Placing her index finger to her lips, Lily whispered, "We're going to escape. Want to come with us?"

The leader frowned. "No. They'll catch you and shoot you. As long as we play music for them we'll be okay."

"Don't tell on us. You'll be back in the camp in your barracks before they find out we're gone. So they won't harm you because they'll never know when we left. You can say we were here cleaning the kitchen."

"All right, hurry."

"This is our chance. Come on, Rachel. Grab your jacket and run. Get into the woods as fast as you can." Lily ran with Rachel until they were both out of breath. "Let's sit for a while."

April 21, 1943

Lily closed her eyes. Before she realized it, she was asleep. A noise woke her. Startled, she shook Rachel. "There's someone in the woods near us."

"Who's out there?" Lily called out.

"It's us. We're freedom fighters. Who are you?"

"We escaped from our work detail at the prisoner camp, Auschwitz. We're looking for help to get back to Warsaw."

"Follow us we're going to the Ghetto to see if we can help them fight the Germans."

"How do you get in there?" Lily asked.

"We have nun habits. We always go at dark so the soldier can't tell we aren't women. The soldiers are still letting the nuns in with food and to help the sick if they're brave enough to enter with the fighting."

"*Pssst. Pssst.* Over here?" Lily heard someone whisper as she walked toward the wire fence. "The nuns told us you were outside."

"It's the boy, John. The one who lent us some clothes."

"Where's Pierre?" Lily asked.

"He was in the Ghetto and escaped through the sewer. He's getting us more ammunition and more men and women to fight."

"What's going on?"

Lily watched him pull wire cutters from his pocket. He made a space wide enough for her and Rachel to fit through.

"Come in. Quick. It's an uprising. The Nazis were going to deport all of us left in the Ghetto to the prison camp. We decided to fight. We started by shooting the collaborators and the Jewish police on April nineteenth. We have gotten ahead of them. They didn't think we could fight. We raised the blue and white flag representing our promised land and the red and white flag of Poland. The Germans are humiliated and are fighting harder."

Lily and Rachel pushed through the opening in the fence and followed the boy as he ran behind the makeshift barricades and bent down in a bunker.

"Here's a gun and some ammunition. It's better you're here than on the streets. You'll be safer. The Germans are so angry with the rebellion they will shoot anything in sight."

Lily looked around as she sat behind the furniture and wood used to slow up bullets and the assault. "Rachel, look at their faces. There was nothing but despair in their eyes the last time we were here. Now there's joy."

"Are you all right, John?"

"Oh yes. We know we probably won't survive, but we'd rather die fighting than in a gas chamber."

Lily shuddered inwardly at the thought of being injured or dying as she and her friend, Rachel, fought alongside the men and women. They took turns eating and sleeping with the fighters. Suddenly she saw the Germans using flame throwers. They set one house after another on fire, driving the inhabitants running out into the street where they were shot to death. Her heart jumped in her chest. The days passed. It was almost May sixteenth. *It's finished.*

"We've got to get out of here. Remember this doesn't end well. Come on, follow me." Lily grabbed her friend's hand. "We're going to escape by…"

"No, not the sewer," Rachel cried.

"It's the sewer or…"

"All right, you don't have to convince me. I want to stay alive."

Lily ran to the middle of a Ghetto street not yet set on fire and pulled off the cover to the sewer. "Okay there's a ladder, it's covered with water. I'll go first. When you start down the ladder, pull the cover back over the opening so none of the soldiers see the open sewer, follow us, or throw a bomb down the hole." Lily stared down the ladder into the sewer. "Ugh. The smell is very bad. Don't breathe deeply." Suddenly it got pitch black. "I'll wait and help you on the last step. Keep your head up. The water is only waist deep."

"How do we know which way to go?"

"Before you put the cover back I looked. There's a tunnel going to the right. The left way looked like it is broken into short passageways. We should go to the right."

"That makes sense. The river is to the right."

"I can't stand this," Rachel said as she propelled her body through the sewer. She let Lily drag her. "I hear the sound of tiny feet scurrying near us. What do you think it is?"

"I'm sure it's rats on the pipes above us. Just keep moving."

"Oh, no. Run." Rachel pushed by her friend and started to run ahead of her.

Lily gripped Rachel's hand, forcing her to slow down.

"Let me out of here." Rachel broke away and ran. The water splashed around her.

"Will you stop? Rachel, the dirty liquid is splashing in my face." Lily wiped her face with the back of her hand. *That did a lot of good, my hand is wet and dirty.*

"Sorry…I can't stand it here, I can't slow down. I have to get out of here. We must be nearing the end."

"I feel cold air. I think we're there." Lily walked fast, pushing the water as she moved. "Ouch. We are at the end. Here's another ladder."

"Be careful, Lily. Peek out and look around when you get to the top."

"There's a street and some bombed out buildings. I see the river. It will only take us a few minutes to reach it. We're in front of it and across the street." Lily reached out and helped her friend climb out of the sewer.

"I'm for swimming with my clothes on in the river. They're filthy. I can smell the horrible odor of the sewer. No one will want to be near us. We're near the convent, aren't we? I'm sure if we can get there without being captured again, we can get the nuns to give us some clothes," Lily said standing near the road.

"Okay. Jump in the river and dunk up and down."

"Get out, I think we're as clean as we're going to get."

"It's about a half mile to the convent and it's dark. No one will see us if we stay close to the bushes. Hurry Lily. Run before we freeze to death."

May 16, 1943

Lily ran. When she reached the iron gate in front of the convent, she stopped to catch her breath. She pulled the bell cord hanging over the gate. Lily watched a nun throw open the door and come hurrying from the sanctuary.

"Yes. What can I do for you? Oh…it's you, Pierre's friend."

"Have the Germans been by tonight?"

"Yes. They've been here and gone a long time ago. Come in, be quick." The nun pushed open the gate.

"Can you give us some clean clothes, please?" Lily smiled.

"Where were you?"

"We were at the Ghetto and escaped by the sewer. We took a dip in the river trying to wash off some of the filth."

"Wait here. There are some Partisans in the barn. They're waiting for their friends and Mother Superior to come back from the Tatras. They will have some clothes for you. They take them off their dead companions and German soldiers." She pushed on a button inside the door.

Lily shivered while she stood in her wet clothes as a nun entered the room.

"Please tell the Partisans to give us two sets of clothes," she said to the nun.

"Girls, get those wet things off. I'll clean them for you. Get under the shower in our quarters. It's in the next room."

"Here you are, Sister."

Lily wrapped in a towel peeked around the open door. She saw one of the Partisans entered the room and handed the nun shirts and jeans.

"Is Mother Superior still in the Tatras?" the Partisan asked.

"The girls would know. Mother told me she was going to meet them. Let me see if they are cleaned up and I'll ask them."

"Mother Superior was going on to Slovakia and didn't need us anymore. We decided to come back to work with Partisans. Right now I want to get some sleep. You can throw away the clothes we came in," Lily said as she changed.

"What's going on at the Ghetto?" Rachel asked.

"The Germans have destroyed the Ghetto in Warsaw. But we saw the Jews fight until finally, they were all dead or escaped. We don't know if Pierre made it out."

"I hope he got out by the sewers like we did," Lily said.

"We heard the general ordered a celebratory event. He blew up the beautiful synagogue built in 1877. It was magnificent. A real landmark for the area. People came from all over to see it."

"Well, you're alive. Maybe you can help build another just as nice. Good night, Sister. Do we still have a bed or mattress in the bell tower?"

"Yes. Go to the sanctuary and up the stairs to bed. I'll wake you tomorrow for breakfast." The sister hurried to the nun's quarters.

Lily turned and looked into the yard of the convent as they walked through the sanctuary to their hiding place.

"Rachel, it's time to leave. Look. Clouds are covering the moon and stars. It's raining. See the mist creeping over the grass. We're going back to our time. Come on." Lily pulled her friend's arm and led her into the raindrops.

October 20, 2014

Lily stood outside the gate of the convent. "I wonder if your car is still on the road. Before we go look at it, I want to see if I can find the tombstone of Mother Superior."

Strolling to the cemetery next to the convent's fenced-in yard, she walked up and down the rows of tombstones. "Here it is. I found it. *Mother Superior-Anna Marie. Abbess, Born in 1906 in Warsaw, Died in 1976 at the convent,*" Lily read out loud. "She lived for thirty years after the war. I wonder how many people she helped to save."

"I don't know, but I bet she's mentioned in the museum in Krakow." Rachel smiled. "Let's go find my car. Hopefully going back in time is over. The last two visits were terrible. I couldn't wait for the bad weather with fog and mists to develop."

"Let's see if it starts," Rachel said when they reached her car.

Lily opened the passenger side door and jumped in. She waited while Rachel pushed the key into the ignition and turned it.

The motor turned over. "I don't believe it. Your car is fine. What happened before? Why did it stop?"

"The only thing I can think of is we were meant to see what we did." Rachel pointed her car toward Kazimierz.

The next day Rachel stood with Lily at the window overlooking the gardens. "I'm so sad it's time for you to go back to France."

"I have to get back to work and Thanksgiving is coming. It's not a French holiday, but my neighbor told me the Americans get together and celebrate. Her brother should be back from his assignment. She promised to introduce me to him. If he isn't, I can wait. I have lots of work to do.

"I'm so glad we've had ten days of sun. It was fun taking you sightseeing. I got to see a lot of things I haven't seen in years."

"And I got to see that all the Nazi war machine has been destroyed and some of the buildings from World War II kept so visitors could see the horror they created. I love the weeds growing in the train tracks of Birkenau where the trains dropped off prisoners to be taken to the gas chambers." She took a deep breath. "I liked the rust of the sign at the entrance of Auschwitz, *Arbeir Macht Frei*, through work freedom. Someday it will fall apart. Best of all we had a hand in helping people escape death."

"One of the sad things was we never saw Pierre after the attack and decimation of the Ghetto in Warsaw. I hope he got away."

"I bet he did. He was pretty good at fooling the enemy."

"I hope so." A tear ran down Lily's cheek. "I would love to know what happened to him."

"Have you slept well since we got back from the 1940s?" Rachel asked.

"A couple of nights I had nightmares. I saw so many of the painful scenes of unthinkable punishment and sadistic Nazis. I heard the music the Nazis played as Jews and others they thought of as undesirables walked to the gas chambers. For a while, I was scared by the flashbacks and didn't want to close my eyes. It got better."

She stared out the living room window. Rain started to spatter on its pane. Fog rolled across the lawn. With a quick glanced around the room, she waited but didn't return to the 1940s. *Going back in time is over for now.* Giving Rachel a hug, she smiled.

"Thank you for a nice visit and right now I'm not going to waste any more time on the bad memories competing for the space the good ones are trying to occupy. I'm going to try to remember our work with the nuns, fighting at the Ghetto, and all the people we met when we got involved with the Partisans." Lily glanced at her watch. "It's time for you to drive me to the train." She hugged her friend again. "It's your turn to visit me in France. Don't forget."

EPILOGUE

Paris, France December 2015

Lily walked through the sanctuary of Notre Dame to the side door and waited until the organist finished his program. She stared up at the stained glass window with biblical scenes. *They're beautiful.* The sunlight coming through the stained glass windows bounced their colors off the silver candle holders and challis sitting on the ornately carved wooden altar. It was the Christmas season and the Cathedral erected on the Île de la Cité a natural island in the middle of the Seine River in Paris stood majestically looking over the city as the daily organ recitals occurred. The building of the Cathedral was started in the eleven hundreds and finished in 1345. There had been much maintenance and restoration through the centuries.

She pushed on the door next to her and strolled into the park and gardens surrounding the Cathedral. The sky was sunny, but the wind picked up since she decided to spend her lunch hour at the Notre Dame's noon holiday concert.

Winter was here. Buttoning her jacket, she wrapped her scarf around her neck as she wandered around the Cathedral grounds. Stopping, she gazed back at the Gothic architecture, bell tower with three hundred and eighty-seven steps, stained glass windows, and gargoyles. *When the weather is nicer, I'll walk to the top and see all of Paris and some of the gargoyles up close.*

Hearing whispering, she turned and looked toward the voices coming from the corner of the garden. *It couldn't be.* What she saw made her eyes widen and her lips parted. A familiar figure stood by a wheelchair next to a cement bench. Even though he bent down talking to the man in the chair, she was sure she recognized the powerful build, the broad shoulders filling his black leather jacket, and his dark brown hair touching the top of his collar. He stood with his hands pushed into the pockets of his jeans. His head tilted down. A pose she remembered belonged to her friend in 1940 Poland.

"Pierre?" she called and watched as the man turned. His skin was bronzed by the wind and sun. The way he slipped on the pair of sunglasses, pushing them to the bridge of his nose, against the rays of the sun. It was the same way he'd made the motion many times when she knew him during World War II. It couldn't be, but the resemblance was too real. Her eyes widened in astonishment. He was so handsome. Her pulse pounded. Her breath caught in her throat and she found herself studying his profile. A warm glow flowed through her.

"No, Charles."

Her brows furrowed in a frown.

He smiled as he turned and stared. His eyes crinkled at their corners.

There it was, the smile and the voice. *I'm imagining things.* She stared. "Sorry…I thought you were someone I used to know." A warmth crept from her chest to her cheeks. "Were you both here for the concert?"

181

"Yes, I'm visiting here with my great-grandfather. His name is Pierre. This is a place he likes to visit so he can hear the special concerts at holiday time. He was part of the diplomatic core during WWII. He helped train and worked with the Partisans in Poland, but always tried to make it back to Paris at this time of year."

Lily watched the elderly man turn and stare at her. Not quite sure what to say, she gave herself a little mental shake.

"Come closer." The elderly man motioned to Lily.

She smiled as she walked slowly toward him. He looked into her face. She still remembered his keen probing eyes and inscrutable expression. "You are lucky you survived," she whispered as she leaned down close to his ear.

She stood and stared at Charles. "Your grandfather looks like someone I've seen in WWII photographs at my friend's house in Poland." *What's a little white lie?*

"He told my sister and me stories when we were young, about the war and his job. Indeed he was lucky he is with us today. He was captured at the end of the war but managed to get back to France when the prison camps were liberated. He married his childhood sweetheart, a French woman, my great-grandmother, and continued in the diplomatic core. I've carried on in his career."

Lily took a few steps back away from the men. Charles was the image of Pierre when he was young. The older man pushed his glasses up on his nose, leaned toward her, and stared again.

"Yes?"

"Young lady, come closer and lean down again so I can study your face." He looked at her as if he were photographing her with his eyes. "What is your name?" He tilted his head at an inquisitive angle and reached up to push a wisp of hair laying on her cheek behind her ear.

She saw the tenderness in his gaze. "My name is Lily."

"I've thought of you through the years. I wondered what happened to you. I came back to the Ghetto. John told me you were there, but with all the fighting I couldn't find you. I'm so glad to see you." Pierre reached for her hand and grasped it.

"Grandfather, you've never met this woman before." He turned toward Lily. "I'm sorry. My grandfather gets confused sometimes."

Lily bent down and whispered in Pierre's ear. "I'm glad you escaped."

"Yes, a group of us got out through the sewer. May fifteenth the day before the rebellion ended we left trying to gather more people to fight and more guns."

When Pierre patted her hand and winked, she smiled and nodded at him. He remembered her.

"We're going to have a glass of wine would you like to join us? My grandson shouldn't let you get away."

"All right, Grandfather. Please." He stared at Lily. "If you don't think I'm being too forward, I would like you to join us," Charles said as he smiled at her.

Her cheeks were warm when her fingers pressed against them. She was sure a rush of pink stained both of them. "I would love to." *Yes, he could have been a young Pierre's twin.* His personality was also the same as his grandfather's. Straightforward and no nonsense. Lily smiled. *When I get to know him, maybe I'll tell him what happened to me on my visit to Poland.* There was a tingling in the pit of her stomach as she found herself studying his profile.

"Charles, don't you think she looks just like your great-grandmother?"

Charles stared at her. "Yes, she could be her twin."

"I think your sister is my neighbor. That's where I've seen you, in a photograph on the side table in her living room. She told me she would introduce us when you came back to Paris."

"Well, that's two people trying to get us together." He laughed.

There was a spark of excitement she couldn't deny. Her heart thumped erratically. Clouds filled the sky. Snow began to fall lightly and collected on the grass as they walked to a café outside the grounds of Cathedral Notre Dame.

As the weeks went by, Lily spent more and more time with Charles. He had not only inherited Pierre's good looks but all of his great-grandfather's good traits. He was adventurous, kind, tender, and loving. In all her letters to her mother and sisters, she told them over and over how close the two of them were getting. She told them all about the concerts, restaurants, and diplomatic functions they attended and how happy she was when Charles helped her critique the restaurants for her column.

Rachel was the first person she told her about Charles, meeting his great-grandfather, and what she discovered about meeting him in Poland when they went back to WWII. "You'll meet him soon," she told her friend. "I would like to see who you think he looks like. I'll send you a photo."

"If I don't hear from you within a few weeks, I'm coming to Paris. I want to meet Charles."

"I promise, I'll send you a photo. We're going to dinner Sunday after we walk the grounds of Notre Dame. We met there. I'll take a photo of him."

"It sounds as if he may have a surprise for you."

"Oh, I don't think so. It's spring and it will be a beautiful day. It's a nice way to spend an afternoon."

The streets were lined with clowns, artists, and mimes. Music filled the air. Spring flowers were in full bloom as she and Charles walked into the gardens of Notre Dame. It was warm when they reached the park.

Lily gazed at the cherry trees in the back corner of the garden. The blossoms were beautiful. The gardens were filled with daffodils, iris, lilies, tulips, and roses in all different colors. Pale pink rose canina climbed the walls at the back of the Cathedral.

They stopped at the bench where he and his grandfather had been the day she met them.

He watched her auburn hair hang gracefully over her shoulders as he pulled her to him.

He gently took her arm and turned her toward him. His large hands took her face and held it tenderly. His nearness was overwhelming. She raised herself on her tiptoes to meet his kiss. He whispered into her hair, "I love you," then pulled away. He kissed her with his eyes then swooped down and captured her lips. When he finally let her go, he smiled.

"Will you marry me?" He took her hand and pressed a kiss into her palm waiting for her reply.

"Yes. Yes. I love you." Her pulse skittered. Her heart pounded. She could barely get through dinner. "Do you think we can get married at Notre Dame?"

"Being a diplomat I can arrange anything."

"Good, it's only right we get married where we met."

"I almost forgot." He pulled a small box from his pocket. When he opened it, Lily saw a large diamond surrounded by sapphires. Her heart fluttered in her chest.

Lily smiled as he put it on her ring finger. "It's beautiful." Tears filled her eyes. "I love you so much."

"Why are you crying?"

"Their tears of joy."

"There's only one problem."

Lily frowned. "What is the problem?"

"I'm getting a new assignment and have to be there at the end of July."

She hesitated. "My mother and sisters will be here as soon as I tell them we're getting married. We have two months. You won't have to do anything except get the groomsman and ushers. They will help me with everything."

They strolled to the restaurant.

Lily noticed that Charles had reserved a window table. A bottle of champagne and two glasses sat on it.

"You haven't eaten very much." Charles stared at her plate."

"I can't eat, I'm too excited." She looked into his eyes and smiled. "I'm going to call my family and tell them to make reservations for Paris."

As soon as she arrived home, she called Rachel and her mother and sisters.

Paris, June 26, 2016

Lily stood in front of the long mirror. Her wedding gown wasn't fussy but very sophisticated with short sleeves and a long train. She picked up her bouquet and smelled the red and white roses as Rachel pinned her veil on her head. Her sisters and Charles' sister stood beside the door smiling. They wore pale blue, full-length dresses that complemented their shades of red hair. Rachel wore lavender enhancing her blond hair.

Lily's mother dressed in a pale green suit. "Where are the children?" she asked.

"They are all playing next door in the yard of the French Embassy."

"Lily, we better start the ceremony before the children get dirty," her mother called to her.

"Yes, Mother. I'm ready to go." Lily smiled as she slipped on her white satin pumps. *I never thought when I took a trip to Poland I would be marrying a French diplomat and the relative of the man I helped save so many Jewish people and enemies of Hitler and the German people.*

"Daisy, please get the children seated and get the music started," Lily said. She set her flowers on the table next to her and pulled on her long white gloves.

She looked out the window and watched the children and Daisy run to the back door of the church. Their feet thumped on the tile floor of the sanctuary. Lily had a special row roped off for them. They would all sit together in the front row of the pews. Lily was sad her father was not there, but she knew he smiled as he looked down on the group with happiness.

When Lily heard the music start, she opened the door and watched each of the girls grab the arm of one of Charles's friend and slowly walk to the altar. Her favorite song, *I will Always Love You* by Whitney Houston played as she waited. When the wedding march began she grabbed her mother's arm and started down the aisle. Lily listened to her mother whine and complain when she heard the wedding would be in Paris. Soon Lily realized it helped when she told her mother she was marrying a diplomat. Her mother was always impressed with a title. She seemed to have a relationship with her mother. Her mother had settled down. Lily smiled. It seemed her mother was enjoying her daughters and grandchildren.

Lily watched Rachel smile and wink at her as she stood at the altar watching Lily walk down the aisle on her mother's arm. Her mother beamed when she handed her to Charles.

Karl knew about what happened on her trip to Poland, but she hadn't told Charles yet, she thought as she stood next to him. She was so happy. *He looks so handsome in his tux.*

He leaned down and smile. Looking up, her heart lurched madly. Lily listened as he started to speak his vows. "…to be my partner, loving what I know of you and trusting what I do not know yet…"

I'll tell him in the South of France as we relax and honeymoon. There have been hints from his great-grandfather so maybe he knows and is waiting for me to talk about it.

She heard his *I do* and after they kissed they hurried down the aisle. They ran from the church and into the garden next to the church as bird seed was thrown at them.

"They're playing your favorite song. Shall we dance?" Charles asked. He stretched his arm across her back and pulled her toward him.

Her heart lurched madly.

When the music stopped, Lily smiled at him. "Would you ask my mother to dance? She seems to be at loose ends without a man."

Lily walked to his great-grandfather, as Charles approached her mother and spun her on the dance floor, and sat next to him.

"You are perfect for my grandson. I'm so happy you are part of our family. Have you told him about going back in time and when we first met?"

"Not yet. I can't seem to find the right time."

"Don't worry. I think he suspects there is something mysterious about you. I believe that's part of what attracts him to you. Do you ever think about Poland and working with the Partisans?"

"Once in a while. I think of how I went back in time and helped so many needy people."

"Pierre," Rachel said. "It's good to see you again." She walked toward her friend. "Lily told me she had seen you again and that Charles is your great-grandson."

"It's good to see you too, Rachel." Pierre gave her a conspiratorial wink. "I'm old, but I can still dance. May I have this one?"

"Lily, your Charles is very special," her mother called as they headed toward her.

"You're right. He is very special." Her heart turned over in response to the heart-rending tenderness of his gaze.

When Charles finished dancing with Lily's mother, he left her with her daughters. He pulled Lily onto the dance floor. Her feet drifted as if she were on a cloud. Her feelings for him intensified. The noise of the music drowned out the thudding of her heart. She looked into his face and her heart lurched madly as he stopped dancing for a moment, held her face gently in his large hands, smiled as he encircled her in his arms, and started to dance again.

Lily smiled. *Life always works out.* She stared at Pierre. *And is never going to be dull with this family.*

A warm shiver went through her and her knees trembled. Her thoughts filtered back to the day she'd met him. She knew there was something special about Charles from the very beginning. He was the image of his grandfather, the man she shared some of World War II with. Her life would be wonderful. She would conquer the good and the bad or whatever life offered and she would do it with her new husband.

THE END

A TASTE OF POLAND

Pierogi

3 cups of flour pour through a sieve makes dough softer and more delicate flavoring
½ teaspoon salt
¾ cup boiling water
¼ cup cold water
½ teaspoon oil

Add salt to flour. Pour boiling water into dry ingredients stir vigorously. Cover bowl with a cloth and set aside for 5 minutes. Add cold water and stir. Cover with a cloth for 15 minutes. Add oil and knead dough until smooth and uniform mass. Roll out dough to about one-tenth of an inch on a floured board. Cut circles with a cup and place filling in the middle. Boil or fry them.

Fillings

Mushrooms – 1-¼ pound assorted mushrooms remove stems and chopped finely. Sauté with ½ Tablespoon butter melted and ½ Tablespoon olive oil. Add ¼ cup minced shallots, 2 Tablespoons lemon juice, 1 teaspoon salt until mixture nearly dry. Add 1 teaspoon thyme and 3 Tablespoons heavy cream. Mix well and fill pierogi in middle and fold over and seal.

Cabbage - steam a cabbage that has been quartered, until tender. Drain and cool. Then squeeze out as much liquid out as possible. Simmer 1 small onion finely chopped in 2 T butter and 2 T chicken broth. Mix 1-½ T cream cheese and 2 t dill. Fill and seal pierogi.

Potato and cheese - Mix 1 cup mashed potatoes, 1 small onions or shallot, 1 ½ t minced sage, egg yolk, and salt to taste. Fill pastry and seal.

Ground Beef - ½ pound ground beef. 1 small onion finely chopped and sauté in 1 T butter, mix with a few shots of gin as you brown the meat. The alcohol will cook away. Fill and seal.

Dessert - use plums or blueberries. 8 cups of fruit. Sugar to taste and 3 T confectioner's sugar. Mix fruit with 1 cup sour cream, ½ t vanilla extract, and ¼ t nutmeg. After pierogis are stuffed and sealed sprinkle with confectioner's sugar.

Did you enjoy *Lily, In Our Mother's Garden, Book Two*? If so, please help us spread the word about Joyce Humphrey Cares and I Heart Book Publishing, LLC.

- Recommend the book to your family and friends

- Post a review on retail sites and Goodreads

- Tweet and Facebook about it

ABOUT THE AUTHOR

Joyce Humphrey Cares lives in Central Florida. A voracious reader since childhood, she finally decided to take a stab at writing. She combines her love of history and the places she has traveled when she weaves her stories.

When she is not writing, Joyce is a Guardian ad litem volunteer, builds and decorates dollhouses, plays golf, and plans her next trip to a place where she can return home and write a romantic suspense or time travel story.

She is a member of Romance Writers of America, Southern State Romance Authors, and the Florida chapter of Mystery Writers of America.

She may be contacted at joycecares01@gmail.com or at her webpage www.joycehumphreycares.com.

Other Books
It Started With Forbidden Love
It Happened Yesterday
Beyond the Mist
Degrees of Wickedness
Violet, In Our Mother's Garden, Book One

Books that appeal to the eye and the heart.

94307611R00124

Made in the USA
Columbia, SC
29 April 2018